PEACHES AND PUCKS

A CHEEKY HOCKEY NOVELLA

M.A. WARDELL

Cataloging-in-Publication data will be on file with the Library of Congress after the publication of the book.

For those who flinched at the sound of a whistle, who sat out the game, who thought sports weren't for you—you were never the problem. You were just waiting for the right team.

AUTHOR'S NOTE

Dear Reader,

This story started as a joke.

No, really. One April Fool's Day, I teased that I was writing a hockey romance—and the internet believed me. When I admitted it was a joke, I swore I'd *never* write one. I mean, me? Hockey? Absolutely not.

Then my friend E'Shel called my bluff. She dared me to write a hockey short story for the *Queers and Quills* anthology—a charity project I couldn't possibly say no to. So I gave in. Just a short story, I told myself.

And then came Darius and Harry.

Somewhere between the quips, the chemistry, and the locker room tension, I fell head over heels for these two. What started as a dare turned into one of the most joyful writing experiences I've ever had. The story kept growing, and before I knew it, that "little hockey short" became *Peaches and Pucks*, a full-blown sweet and spicy novella about finding love in the most unexpected places.

So, to everyone who thought I couldn't—or wouldn't

—write a hockey romance: you were right... until you weren't.

All my best,
    M.A. Wardell
    (Matt)

CONTENT WARNINGS

Peaches and Pucks is a sweet, low-angst story, but here are the content warnings if you need them.

An MC struggling with insecurities related to being gay in hyper-masculine athletic spaces, hole-in-the-wall restaurants, a dudebro who's a secret romantic, kisses on the cheek, taking shots on and off the ice, armpit and jockstrap kink, and mentions of elementary school students playing recorders and boomwhackers

Harry

1

HARRY

I'M NOT ENTIRELY sure how I ended up on a stuffy chartered motorcoach surrounded by Sharks. That would be *the* Sharks, the boisterous fifth-grade boys' hockey team from the school I teach at. Yet here I am.

The less-than-luxurious bus chugs down the interstate, transporting us to picturesque Warwick, Rhode Island—site of the New England Peewee Hockey Division Three semifinals. The fact that I know any of those words is something my father would take pride in. Mainly because the only sport I ever entertained as a child was hiding in the back of gym class, hoping to be picked last for any team and then knowing I'd be placed in whatever position required the least amount of athletic skill. Way back in right field, staring at the clouds? Keeping the bench warm while the taller, more svelte guys played basketball? Collecting the misfired and out-of-bounds balls on the tennis court? I'm your guy. I have zero knowledge or interest in hockey and would prefer to keep it that way.

As a fifth-grade language arts teacher at Crossroads Elementary, my only extracurricular duties include working with Christine Wong, the music teacher, on the musical each year. We closed *Into the Woods JR.* two weeks ago to rave reviews. It's identical to the regular version, except it completely removes the entire tragic second act. Nobody missed the death and despair. Go figure.

"Peterson, you alive?" Darius Hill—Coach Hill to the boys on the bus—asks. He's the PE teacher at Crossroads and the one person who makes my life uncomfortable at school.

"All good," I say.

I force a grin and hold up my worn copy of *Lord of the Flies*. Regardless of my previous interactions with Darius, William Golding's classic will be the only tension between civility and chaos on this overnight hellscape of a trip I was roped into.

I'm not sure what I ever did to him, but the tension in the air is palpable whenever he's around. Maybe it's my lack of sports knowledge beyond women's figure skating and the occasional leer at men's tennis because of those thick thighs in short shorts . . . or my disinterest in his lunchtime fantasy football conversations in the teacher's lounge . . . or the fact that I love to suck dick.

From the moment I was hired, Darius Hill has made it abundantly clear he doesn't like me.

"Thanks again," he says from three uncomfortable inches away.

We're crammed into the only vacant seats near the back of the bus, him against the window while I've got the aisle—right next to the bathroom that vaguely smells like an overused outhouse at a hot dog eating contest.

"No problem."

Except it is a problem. I'm not supposed to be here. I should be home in bed, eating ice cream from the container while watching the new season of that show about a ridiculously attractive American woman who moves to Paris and spends her time eating delicious food and fawning over gorgeous French men—none of whom have any interest in sports.

"I never took you for a guy to take a dare," Darius says.

My eyes are fixed on the screen four seats ahead of us playing *Despicable Me 4*, which is completely lost on me since I've never seen *Despicable Me 1-3* or any of the *Minions* movies. It's really all drivel that works well, even without my headphones plugged into the seat for sound, and I try to get lost in the Minion playing a banana like a saxophone. As my grandmother would say, *this isn't great theatre, Harry.*

But I can see Darius in my peripheral vision, wearing the Bruins cap that's apparently superglued to his scalp and burning a hole into the side of my head with his light hazel eyes. His face is adorned with scruff that seems to defy time, always maintaining the same perfect length by some inexplicable straight-boy sorcery.

"I'm not here for a dare." I keep my eyes focused on the chaotic little yellow people.

"Oh? Why, then?"

I face Darius, taking in the athletic suit with his name

emblazoned on the chest. My eyes dart down to 'Coach Hill' stitched over his firm pec, taunting me.

"I'm here for the kids." I nod at the group of boys on the bus.

Most of them are plugged in, laughing at the immature animated antics. Fifth-grade boys are interesting animals. Developmentally, they're typically behind their female counterparts. Smaller. Less aware of the world around them. In a few months, the total onslaught of body odor will be in full effect, and I'll be forced to deliver my dreaded 'personal hygiene' chat to them. It's that or cosplay as Esther Williams and wear a nose plug to avoid the ripe onion smell while attempting to teach the intricacies of *Treasure Island*.

Darius raises his right eyebrow. He's a cocky motherfucker. I refuse to lower myself to his level and take the bait. As Michelle Obama says, "When they go low, we go high." *God, I wish I had her arms.*

I lift my chin, meet his gaze, and continue.

"Without another staff chaperone, the trip would be canceled. It's not the boys' fault Mr. Applegate's dog went into labor and he had to take her to the emergency vet in New Hampshire. He didn't even know she was expecting. A surprise poodle pregnancy. You can't make this stuff up." I shrug. "And I was . . ."

"Available."

As Darius smirks, a surge of frustration pulses through me, my hand involuntarily twitching with the overwhelming desire to wipe that smug expression off his face.

"I was in the office. Mrs. Stephen was in full panic

mode. I wasn't letting her take the hit. She's mere months away from retirement. There was no way I was making her ride the bus to Rhode Island with a group of fifth graders and . . . you. It was my civic duty to step up."

"And you were available."

"Yes. I didn't have any plans on a Friday night. Sue me."

"You did a nice thing, Peterson."

"Thank you."

I pull my lips in, the corners of my mouth tightening, while my fingers glide through my hair, untangling the knots. My curls are becoming wild and untamed. I need to schedule a trim.

"I never knew you had an interest in hockey. We don't read musty books." He flicks the tattered cover in my lap. "Or break out into song mid-thought like those fairy-tale characters."

I leer at him, and if I were in an old-timey cartoon, I'm relatively certain smoke would be billowing out of my ears.

"You're right—zero interest in anything related to pucks. Delightful fairy from *A Midsummer Night's Dream* aside. I'm here because Johnny Rodriguez gave me his best sad puppy dog eyes about the team not being able to play in the semifinals because of Mr. Applegate's unexpected visit from the canine stork."

"Mrs. Stephen would've come. She's done it before. She actually enjoys hockey."

Darius pulls his baseball hat up, exposing the tiniest bit of his dark brown hair at the top of his head. The man lives in a cap. In the four years I've been at Crossroads,

I've only seen him without it once. Once. When that chipmunk wrangled its way in through the girl's locker room and he used his hat to scoop it up and bring it outside. What a fucking hero.

"I think you're curious," he continues, his eyes lingering a little too long on my face for my comfort. "About . . . hockey. You know I play on an adult team, too. If you're genuinely interested."

The shit-eating grin reappears, and once again, I'm back in middle school, being taunted by the boys on the playground. Except now, the boy is wearing a full-grown human costume.

"Hockey?" I ask, quickly lowering my voice to make sure any boys awake and not plugged in don't hear me question the reason we're headed to The Ocean State on a rickety, out-of-commission tour bus.

"A bunch of angry men with too much testosterone banging into each other and hitting each other with sticks? Sounds positively dignified."

Darius huffs, and his nostrils flare. He has the most perfect nose on that annoying face, and how dare he have sexy nostrils too?

"You're not interested in a bunch of dudes swinging our sticks back and forth?"

"Will you keep it down? And stop," I whisper-shout. "There's no need to be inappropriate."

Darius stands, holding on to the ledge of the overhead railing.

"We're almost at the rink. I need to move to the front of the bus."

Before I can rise or move over, he shimmies in front of

me. The dark navy and—I'm guessing—polyester blend of his workout pants passes inches in front of my face. His bulge comes dangerously close, and I'm tempted to punch him in the dick.

"Me? Inappropriate?" he asks, standing in the aisle. "We have to share a room tonight, Peterson. I'd never think of it."

Darius winks and walks toward the driver. His plump ass looks like two soccer balls in his damn athletic wear. And now I'm making improper sports references.

The bus veers off the highway, and a mix of excitement and nervousness blankets me as we approach the rink.

2

———

HARRY

AS WE DRIVE into downtown Warwick, the streets are lined with mature trees and historic brick buildings. A picturesque town square serves as the heart of the area, featuring what appears to be a centuries-old town hall with a clock tower. Marty McFly would feel right at home.

The Mighty Moose Commemorative Ice Rink takes up an entire block, and I wonder what had to be torn down to make room for it. There's nothing mighty about it, and I'm not exactly sure what it commemorates. I'm not sure if the moose population in Rhode Island rivals ours in Maine, but maybe it's a good sign about the game. Set? Match? I have no idea.

"Mr. Peterson, whaddya think?" Johnny asks.

With thick glasses strapped to his face by a lime-green athletic band that appears to be squeezing his poor head like a boa constrictor, Johnny peers up at me, and I remember I'm supposed to sound interested.

"The ice looks cold."

"Good one, Mr. P.," Victor Henson says.

Victor is almost a foot taller than Johnny, and when he wraps his arm around his shoulder, he misses it and ends up grabbing him by the neck. Based on Johnny's reaction, he's either used to it, doesn't mind, or both.

"Yeah, good one."

Johnny and Victor join the rest of the boys and head over to what appears to be our team's designated area. I think it's called a dugout. Or maybe that's for football. Or maybe I'm just confusing it with a secret hideout for superheroes.

Scanning the arena, I quickly identify a cozy spot a few rows back where I can sit and catch up with my book while the boys unpack their bags of gear.

"Think fast!"

Oof. Something hits me in the middle of my chest. Hard.

"Mother of pearl!" The words come flying out before I can think, and the impact of whatever hit me registers. My eyes land on the culprit—a black disc lies at my feet.

"You were supposed to catch it," Darius says.

"I told you, I'm here as a chaperone only. Why are you lobbing sports paraphernalia at me?"

"It's called a puck. Come on, Peterson. You're not getting off that easy."

Coach Hill hooks his arm in mine and drags me toward the dugout superhero area, where the boys are already unpacking and covering their bodies with various pads. My elbow leads the rest of my body as he tugs me along, and why does he take such delight in tormenting me?

"I was going to sit over there and read until the game's over," I say, eyeing the seat I was heading for a few rows up.

"And miss all the action?"

His hand rests just over my chest, and he slaps me three times.

"No way. The boys and I need your help. Right, team?"

"Right, Coach!"

I'm not exactly sure if they've heard him or are conditioned to give that response whenever he asks a question.

"Mr. Peterson," Johnny says, "Coach Applegate usually sets up the cones for warm-up drills, gathers the pucks, and runs the penalty kill and defense."

I blink a few times, trying to decipher the nonsensical words he's uttering.

"I have no idea what any of that means," I say with a shrug.

"Sit here."

Darius's hands are on my shoulders, guiding me to the end of a long wooden bench overlooking the rink. When he gets me where he wants me, he pushes down, and my ass hits the hard surface.

"Just watch. Listen. Got it, Coach?"

"I'm not . . ."

"When you're here"—he points to the ice—"with them, you're Coach Peterson."

My mouth opens, but nothing comes out. Darius Hill has rendered me speechless. I'm tempted to retrieve the novel from my satchel. I'm tabbing character arcs for the coming week's lessons. My intention is to highlight the flaws and explore how they influence character motivations, propelling the plot forward. I think it'll help students with their writing as well.

A loud whistle interrupts my train of thought. The metallic culprit falls from Darius's plump lips and bounces against his sternum. When I catch his gaze, his mischievous wink sends a flurry of butterflies fluttering in my stomach, and my eyes dart away.

He's giving directions, yelling in that PE teacher way that mostly sounds like he's screaming, but the kids don't seem bothered in the least, and I surmise this must be how he regularly communicates with them.

Victor and Craig skate onto the ice, plopping orange cones down. Before I can take my book out and resume tabbing, the rest of the boys flood the ice, skating around them with their sticks and pushing pucks around. There's an almost balletic quality to the entire endeavor, and I wonder if any of them have ever seen *Swan Lake*.

Next to me on the bench, Darius finishes lacing up his skates and rises. He doesn't wobble or hold on for balance; he simply stands above his blades. Before he joins the boys, he turns and says, "Maybe if you can keep your nose out of that book for a minute, you'll learn something. I'll quiz you later in the hotel room."

He winks, turns, and zooms off. Heat flashes from my chest, creeping up my neck, and overtaking my face. Is Darius Hill flirting with me?

AS THE GAME FINALLY TRANSPIRES, the boys—whom I've wrangled into their desks and convinced to sit still for close to an hour at a time, often reading silently while barely moving—create a blur of motion on the ice, all centered on a puck that, truth be told, I can barely see.

I started the game staring at the giant clock above the rink, watching it to determine when this would all end so I might grab some peaceful reading time back in the hotel before returning to the bus in the morning and heading home. But as play progresses, I find myself drawn to the vim and vigor of the boys.

Johnny sits next to me, doing his best to explain the basics of play. I make a joke about wishing the Sharks were playing the Jets instead of the Otters, but it flies right over poor Johnny's head.

"When do you get a turn?" I ask.

"Oh, Coach doesn't put me in," Johnny replies. "But it's okay. I'm not very good. I just like practicing and being part of the team."

My mind flashes back to being ten, watching my father and brothers play football on Thanksgiving morning. Wanting to be included but also petrified of playing. Running inside to help my mother in the kitchen.

I know enough from Johnny's explanation to know we're in the last period, and if our team doesn't get the tiny black disc into the opposing team's goal, we lose. If we can score, it will be a tie, and both teams will advance to the next round. Johnny said something about that being a peewee rule, and in the NHL, there's overtime that sometimes can last a really long time. I'm grateful we're not facing that possible scenario.

But now that the game is almost over, and the Sharks are down 1-0, my heart races in anticipation of the loss.

"Well, that's it." Darius plops down on the bench, sandwiching Johnny between us. He's been on his feet the entire time, pacing, smacking his gum, screaming, and huddling with the boys. He has a mini whiteboard he's used to scribble what Johnny explains are plays but that the boys never seem to execute as instructed. If nothing else, the entire experience has been entertaining.

"There's still a minute left in the period," I say, nodding toward the giant timepiece with a satisfied grin. I pay attention. I can read a digital clock. I know a single term related to the event!

Darius looks at me, his big hazel eyes wide, and for the first time, his confidence seems to wane. His hand grips Johnny's leg over the padding of his hockey pants, and I finally get it. Darius and I share the same motive for being here. The boys. I'm here so they can play. He's here so they can win.

"It's okay, Coach. We tried our best," Johnny says. He puts his hand on Darius's, and witnessing this tender moment between them sparks something in me.

"But there's still a minute left," I say. "Well, forty-five seconds now. We just need one touchdown."

"Goal," Johnny says.

"Goal. Basket. Touchdown. It's all semantics. Coach Hill, surely we can wrangle a home run from these boys."

Darius's gaze meets mine, and he blinks, pulling his lips in and nodding slowly.

"You're right. We're not rolling over and giving up.

We're the Sharks. If we're going down, we're going down fighting."

He stands, leans over the railing to the rink, raises his right hand, and shouts, "Timeout!"

The referee blows his whistle, and the Sharks scurry off the ice and onto the bench. Shoulders are slumped. Chins are down. The boys seem well aware that this marks the end of their run for the season.

Next year, they'll be off to middle school, where they'll transform into Wildcats. Over one summer, they'll leave the ocean, grow four legs, and become entirely different animals. This was their swan song. Their shark song, so to speak. I don't think sharks sing, but I'm not a science teacher—I'll have to ask Mr. Butters.

"Sharks. We have . . ." Darius glances up at the clock that stands frozen for the moment. "Forty-two seconds. I'm not expecting a miracle, but we didn't drive all the way to Rhode Island to not give it our all."

As I sit on the bench, a smile crosses my face as I observe him pacing back and forth, pouring his heart into the pep talk for the sullen boys.

"I know I don't teach math, but let me tell you—you miss one hundred percent of the shots you don't take." He pulls in a quick breath. "Johnny, I'm tapping you in."

Johnny's eyes almost pop out of his head, and I wrap my arm around him, giving him a silent squeeze of support.

"But . . ." Johnny isn't able to finish before Darius interrupts.

"But nothing. You've got this, Rodriguez. Go out there, and take your shot. You've got nothing to lose."

"Except the game, and our spot in the finals," Victor says matter-of-factly.

"True," Darius replies. "But we've got this. Team, I want you to back Johnny up. Don't let those Otters near him."

Darius flashes his whiteboard. There's a drawing, and he's scribbling, making arrows all over the place as he talks with complete determination on his face.

"Craig and Nicholas, lure them away, create a distraction. Protect the puck. Then Johnny can take his shot. Their goalie is tired. I saw him yawning. Shoot on the outside."

There's more scrawling on the board, and the boys nod their heads, their pre-game liveliness returning.

"Okay, let's do this, Sharks!" Darius shouts.

The team calls back "Go, Sharks!" and they skate out onto the ice.

I don't remember standing, but I'm next to Darius, leaning over the ice, watching the boys take their places as the referee blows his whistle, and they take off in a gust. I do my best to keep my focus on Johnny. He's smaller than everyone else on the ice, but when Benji hurls the puck at him, he manages to keep it away from the Otters—mostly because, just as Darius instructed, Craig and Nicholas skate circles around anyone who comes close, diverting them from stealing the prize.

When I glance up at the clock, it flashes twenty, and the loud, obnoxious buzzer that ended the first two sessions is imminent. Johnny seems to know it's now or never. He skates across the ice, passing about fifteen feet from the goalie, who tracks him with his mask-covered face.

Johnny pulls his stick back, about to shoot, and the goalie falls on his knees, holding his armored hands high, ready to block—but nothing happens. Johnny skillfully maneuvers the puck forward, deceiving the goalie with a swift move before effortlessly propelling it into the other side of the net.

Screams fill the air as the boys go wild, jumping and piling onto Johnny, making it impossible for me to see him anymore.

"Fuck, yes!" Darius screams, and I hope the boys don't hear their PE teacher and coach using such foul language over the roar in the rink.

"He did it. He fucking did it!" Darius grabs my shoulders and pulls me into a huge embrace, lifting me off the floor and tossing me back and forth like a rag doll. I'm lightheaded, and I'm not sure if it's from being off the ground, the shaking, or being plastered against Darius's frame. Even through his track jacket, the firmness of his chest sends a jolt of intensity through my body.

The boys chant, "Coach, Coach, Coach," and Darius lowers me. For a split second, my face comes closer to his than I expect, his warm peppermint breath blowing the curls off my forehead before he turns and joins his team on the ice.

I remain on the safe, non-slippery ground, experiencing a surge of gratification as I witness the team surrounding him with affection. A smile bursts across my face, and a sense of pride swells within me. Contrary to everything I've believed my entire life, maybe sports aren't so bad after all.

3

HARRY

AFTER A CELEBRATORY MEAL at the local pancake and waffle establishment where the team carb loads while Darius makes a face at my Cobb salad with low-fat dressing on the side, we finally arrive at the Vacation Inn. We aren't vacationing, and it barely resembles an inn, so I don't have high hopes for a luxury spa or mints on my pillow.

Darius heads to the counter to check us in, while I hang back in what I think is supposed to be a lobby with the boys and the few parents who have joined us.

Everything is mustard yellow or some horrid shade of brown, but these ten-year-old boys don't seem to care about such things. Filled with elation from the tie that ensured the Sharks' continued participation in the tournament, and having indulged in heaps of pancakes and an assortment of sweet desserts for dinner, they're a content, albeit rowdy, group.

The school reserves rooms with two queen beds, and three to four boys will be in each. The few parents that drove separately will provide help. Darius and I will share a room, and I've brought my eye mask and noise-canceling headphones to give myself some semblance of privacy from him making straight guy noises in the other bed. After the wink, embrace, and too-close-for-comfort encounter at the rink, I ponder splurging for my own room, but then I remember the forty-seven dollars in my checking account and realize the two beds will have to suffice.

"All set," Darius says, walking over to join us. He hands me a paper with the room numbers listed and a stack of key cards.

"I'll take the left, you take the right, and we'll meet back in our room." He winks, and no, sir, we will be having none of that.

After I make sure the eight boys assigned to me are settled in their two rooms, I head to the end of the hallway to 309. The door is ajar, and when I walk in, I'm smacked in the face by the king-sized bed resting in the middle of the poorly appointed room.

"Yeah, so they only had four doubles and a single, and I figured it made more sense for us to take this room than ask four boys to share a bed. You're cool with that, right?"

Without unzipping it, Darius pulls his Sharks hoodie over his head, the T-shirt underneath coming off with it . . . and within two minutes, we're sharing a bed and he's shirtless.

"Um. Sure."

Darius Hill, who reminds me of the boys in middle school who called me a fairy before I knew I was one, stands half-naked before me. His chest, firm but not overly muscular, with only a dusting of soft brown hair that matches the longest strands on top of his buzzed head, taunts me. The movement in my khakis alarms me because I'm not supposed to be here. And yet, somehow I find myself in a distant state, far from home, with an almost undressed Coach Hill.

"Cool. I'm going to take a quick shower. You don't need to wait up."

He turns around and pulls his pants and underwear off in one fell swoop before adding, "Unless you want."

His ass, like two perfect globes, sways back and forth as he heads into the yellow-and-tan bathroom. What is it with the Vacation Inn and earth tones?

Okay—we're sharing this bed. He's naked—you kind of need to be for a shower. I give myself a quick sniff. I'm clean enough. I did little but sit on a bus and then a bench. I casually throw my bag onto the worn-out chair near the old desk, and its creaking echoes through the room. Knowing we'd be sharing a room, I brought pajamas. There's no way I'm sleeping in my usual undershirt and boxer briefs in the same room as Coach Darius Hill, let alone the same bed. Maybe I should've rented a suit of armor—and a chastity belt. You know, just in case my evening plans involved a jousting tournament or attempting to keep my quickly growing erection hidden.

Removing my books, clothes for tomorrow, and toiletry bag, I procure my pj's from the bottom of my small duffel. It's fine. I can put some of the extra pillows I spied in the closet in between us and hug the edge of the bed. I'm guessing Darius will be asleep in minutes, and I'll just pop my headphones in and listen to the *Moby*

Dick audiobook. Or maybe another classic would be a better choice.

I quickly undress down to my underwear and pop on the soft poly-cotton blend shirt. As I'm pulling the pants on, I hear Darius from behind me.

"Oh, he's got fancy underwear. Very nice."

I take a deep inhale, turn around, and glare. My heart races, and I try to ignore the fiery heat crawling up my neck like a rogue flame, daring me to surrender.

"These are Old Navy. They're not fancy. Or expensive."

And then I realize he's only wearing a towel. A hotel towel. It's small, thin, and doesn't leave much to the imagination. I can see nearly everything beneath the flimsy excuse for a cover-up. If this were a decent establishment, they'd be large, plush, and not allow the outline of his cock to be so clear. Fuck my life.

"I said they're nice. Learn to take a compliment, Harry."

His use of my first name—for the first time ever—pushes the heat from my face back down my torso and right to my groin. I quickly pull my pajama pants up.

"Did you want to shower?"

"No, I'm good. Still fresh and clean."

I give a feeble smile.

"Well, the bathroom is all yours. I'm ready to hit the hay."

And then Darius walks around to the other side of the bed and throws his towel on the chair like yesterday's news.

He's a blur as he dives under the covers, frantically

arranging the pillows behind his head. With his hands propped up, his biceps tense, and his armpits exposed, every muscle screams for attention. Dear God, what am I supposed to do now?

As I brush my teeth, I go over the situation in my head. Darius Hill is straight. Or I thought he was—is. Darius Hill is an asshole who torments me and attempts to make my life hell at school. He's also incredibly sexy. And naked. And in the bed we're about to share for the night.

I can do this. I worked in an ice cream store as a teenager and barely ate anything. After a few months, I wasn't even hungry for ice cream. And they had the best mint chip—not those tiny flakes of chocolate, but giant, full-sized chips. If I can resist the allure of minty, chocolaty-sweet frozen dessert, I can resist spending a night in bed with a PE teacher-slash-hockey coach who I'm almost certain doesn't even like men.

With a steeling breath, I open the door and march to my side of the bed. I avoid making eye contact as I crawl under the covers and turn my body away from him, quickly securing my eye mask in place. I'm like a horse with blinders—out of sight, out of mind. Take that, clean, naked man emanating heat a mere two feet away.

"You good if I turn the lights off?"

I've never heard Darius's voice so soft. It's like the bus ride, intense game, and hot shower somehow put a damper on his volume. He almost sounds . . . sweet.

"Mm-hmm."

Maybe if I keep my communication to wordless affirmations, he'll doze off and leave me alone. I hear the light click and begin counting breaths, hoping sleep will come.

"Thanks again for coming," he whispers. "It meant a lot to the boys."

"Yup," I say. The boys. The only reason I'm here.

Technically, it's a word, but only one—no more.

"And me."

I hear some rustling and the sheets shifting, but I stay as still as a fly caught in a spider's web.

It's quiet for a minute, only the sound of our breathing and my heart pounding against my ribcage in my ears.

And then, Darius speaks.

"Listen, Harry, I know you think I'm a Neanderthal jerk—and, well, you're not completely wrong. I don't mean to be so gruff with you. I swear I'm not a complete asshole." He shifts, and there's a gentle tug at the sheets. "It's just a cover. I hope you can forgive me. No hard feelings. Anyway, thanks again for coming."

"A cover for what?"

Darius takes a few slow, deep breaths, making me uncertain if he'll respond. However, his soft voice eventually breaks the silence.

"Have you ever seen one of the boys teasing a girl in class? Making jokes. Doing all he can to make her miserable?"

I'm not positive, but it sounds like he's on his back, facing the ceiling. His shoulder can't be more than six inches from me. The warmth from his skin almost reaches my back.

"Yeah. Victor is horrible to Rebecca Norwood. I've had to chat with him about it. Twice."

"Same. The teasing in PE can be brutal." He takes a deep sigh. "Why do you think he does it?"

I flip over to face him, and tug my eye mask off. "He likes her. Obviously."

As soon as the words leave my mouth, I understand what Darius is trying to tell me. Or I think I do.

"Wait, so you're telling me you have the maturity of a ten-year-old boy?"

He shrugs, sticks his tongue out, and makes a slow fart noise. This doesn't bode well for me.

When he finishes with the raspberry, I say, "But you're straight."

"Says who?"

The bright lights of the parking lot creep through the drawn curtain enough so I can make out his silhouette—he's still staring at the ceiling.

"You're the PE teacher. You love sports. You coach hockey, and you . . . yell—all the time. I'm not sure I've ever seen you without a baseball hat until ten minutes ago when you got naked in front of me."

"So you make assumptions about people based on societal norms about things like clothes and sports. Got it."

"Well, didn't you assume I'm gay because I teach English and co-direct the musical every year?"

"No, Harry. I didn't. I *knew* you were gay because the first time you ate in the teacher's lounge, you and Christine had an entire conversation about which Marvel character you'd like to fuck, and you, not surprisingly, picked Wolverine."

"That doesn't make me gay. Most straight guys would do Wolverine."

He lets out a small laugh, and how the hell did I miss this about him?

"You're not wrong, but it was a pretty good indicator."

"And who would yours be?" I ask.

I'm on the edge of a cliff, waiting to jump, as I watch his lips and wait for his answer.

"That's a no-brainer. Spiderman. But mostly for Peter Parker. I like someone smart. Someone who reads lots of books. A real nerd. That's hot as fuck."

"Really?" I'm up on one elbow now. "Not Iceman? You literally coach ice hockey." He's quiet, so I lie on my back next to him, keeping those few precious inches between us. "Seemed like an obvious choice."

"Nope." Now Darius props himself up on an elbow, facing me. As his warm, minty breath grazes my chin, I can't help but feel a surge of anticipation, causing my pajama pants to tighten. "I'm always going for the geek."

And with that, Darius brushes the curls away from my forehead and moves his face closer. He's watching me, and while I'm not sure what's unfolding, I'm strangely at ease with it.

4

HARRY

"JUST TO BE CLEAR, Spiderman and not . . . Jean Grey? She can read minds. That's got to come in handy."

"Nope." He moves a rogue curl away, keeping his hand on my head. My heart pounds with such intensity, I fear it may rupture through my ribcage.

"Storm? Anyone who can change the weather on a whim would get my vote. We could have snow days on demand."

"Uh-uh."

"Black Widow? Scarlett Johansson has made me question my sexuality on multiple occasions. I'm not even a massive Marvel fan, and I streamed that movie three times because of her."

His finger traces down my jawline. I think it's his thumb, and it lands right under my bottom lip. Darius moves closer, his face only inches from mine.

"If you don't stop talking, Harry, I'll have no choice but to kiss you to shut you up."

I open my mouth, maybe to protest or call his bluff by

saying more, but nothing comes out because Darius's lips, full and soft, still tasting like peppermint toothpaste, brush mine. He's tentative, gentle, even, and a soft moan escapes my mouth because never in a million years did I expect my impulse decision to chaperone the fifth-grade boys' hockey team would lead me to kiss a naked Coach Hill in an only-one-bed situation.

Or maybe, deep down, a part of me hoped for this. I must have seen the parallels between his behavior and Victor's with Rebecca—not consciously, but on some level. My head spins, but before I'm able to continue overthinking how I ended up in a hotel bed with him, Darius pauses the kiss and asks, "Is this okay?"

"So now you're concerned with my feelings?"

He nods, and fuck my life.

"Yes, Harry. Consent is hot. Don't they teach that in all those books you read?"

I open my mouth to reply, but—I'm speechless. Please let his mouth find its way back to mine and never stop kissing me. I grab the back of his head, and the peach fuzz of his buzz cut tickles my palm as I pull him in, deepening the kiss and poking my tongue at his lips.

Darius rolls on top of me, his hot skin still damp from the shower. Or maybe he's sweating. Either way, my fingers find his strong back muscles and hold him in place as his tongue slips into my mouth with a groan. He fucking groans and something inside me melts.

And then I realize—Darius is rock hard, and he's trying to hold his midsection off me to avoid me feeling the full force of what he's packing.

"Darius?" We're still kissing, and the word tumbles into his mouth. He pulls back and searches my face.

"What's wrong?"

"Nothing. Just . . ." I reach down and grab his waist, pulling him down. His stiffness grinds into mine, confined under my pajamas. When I notice his bottom lip quivering, I suck it into my mouth. "There."

"You sure?"

Yup, he's right. Asking for consent is hot. My hand moves between us, his thick cock full in my hand, the heat sending a wave of desire to my core, and I gently squeeze, allowing my fingers to make out what I had only glimpsed before. The tip is sticky with precum, and I'm pretty confident there's nothing more I want than to have it filling my mouth. Soon.

"Okay. Mr. Peterson is sure," he says, and his tongue resumes excavating the inside of my mouth.

Darius ruts into my palm, and my other hand joins the first, massaging his lower stomach, feeling the happy trail that leads from his belly button to his rather full bush. I'm imagining how far I can deep-throat Coach Hill when everything suddenly stops, and he rolls off me.

Before I can ask what's wrong, he says, "Pajamas off."

"Oh, he's bossy now."

"Hey, I'm the coach."

"Yes, sir."

I quickly push my pants down, my dick springing up against my stomach, and as I attempt to remove them completely, Darius grabs the waistband and yanks.

"Okay." I take his hand, wanting him to return to kissing me, but he doesn't budge. Instead, he pulls at the hem of my pajama shirt, and taking his cue, I lift my arms so he can remove it. When I'm completely naked, he finally returns, and the feeling of his heated skin on mine electrifies my senses. If this is my reward for attending a hockey game, I might just have to start scouting for a Zamboni of my own.

"Fuck, I've wanted to do this for a long time." His lips are close to mine, and each word sends his hot breath over my face.

"Do what?"

"This." He kisses me softly.

His fingers wrap around my shoulders, squeezing.

"And this." A soft thrust of his cock on mine.

Darius can't be more than ten pounds heavier than I am, but his weight on me makes my blood boil. He brushes his hands through my hair, getting lost in the curls as our tongues resume playing the only sport I know well—tonsil hockey.

I'm doing my best to stroke him between our bodies, but it's not easy. When he pulls back to catch his breath, heeding his advice to the team, I take my shot.

"Darius, I need you in my mouth. Now."

Just as he moves in to resume kissing, I gently draw away.

"Not that. This." I give his cock a gentle squeeze and brush my thumb over the tip, spreading the precum over his entire head.

"Oh."

"Is that okay?"

"Yeah. Sure." He moves off me. "I mean, duh. Of course it's okay. I didn't want to pressure you, is all."

"Darius Hill." I kiss his chin. "I want you to sit in that chair for me."

I hop out of bed, toss my bag onto the floor, and pat the seat. Darius joins me and sits, spreading his legs wide. I move to my knees and take him in my hand, jerking him a few times, and yup, he's hard and ready.

"Now, just relax and enjoy this," I say.

Darius's fingers brush against my cheek before sliding into my hair, his grip tightening as he holds on for the ride I'm about to give him.

I lick near the base of his shaft, and I give his balls a little kiss before gliding up to the head. He's leaking precum, and the salty-sweetness entices me. "Someone's excited."

"Fuck yeah, I am." He pulses his cock in my hand, the heat palpable. "I've been dreaming about this for . . . years."

"Are you ready to get sucked, Coach?"

When I glance up at him, Darius nods eagerly, like he's been waiting for this his entire life.

I take his head in slowly, licking around the tip, giving every spot attention. I'm not going to just start sucking and bobbing like some uncouth heathen. This mouthwatering cock deserves to be savored.

When he lifts his hips, I place a hand on his chest and pull off. "Easy. Give me a minute to appreciate this." Holding him with my other hand, I notice more precum escaping the tip. I clean it off with my tongue, and Darius shudders under me.

"You'll get to fuck my mouth soon. I promise."

"Holy shit, Harry."

I laugh and take as much of him in as I can. He's not much bigger than me, but I'm not trying to choke within the first few seconds of blowing him. There's plenty of time for that.

When I've almost reached the base, his soft pubic hair brushes the bridge of my nose. My hand on his chest finds his nipple, and I begin playing with it. Between having his cock and chest attended to, Darius's breathing becomes heavy and slow.

"Harry. When you're not yapping, that mouth of yours is magic."

After a few more bobs on his glorious cock, I pull off. I need more.

The image of him naked, walking into the bathroom flashes in my head. That round, perfect butt. So damn delectable.

"Have you ever had your ass eaten?"

Darius's eyes go wide.

"I'll take that as a no."

I stand, pull him up, and he wraps his arms around me. We're almost the same height, but I'm about half an inch taller, and Darius immediately returns to kissing me. His tongue brushes the inside of my mouth, he's grabbing at my ass, and well, this entire encounter wasn't planned, so we'll be keeping things to oral, but who knows, depending on how things work out, maybe someday we'll rail each other.

I reach around and give his ass a squeeze. "Now, let's have you kneel over the chair."

His mouth drops open a little as I turn him around,

but he complies with my command, positioning his forearms comfortably on the mesh seat.

I lower myself and gently tap his inner thigh, feeling the warmth of his skin. As I graze the light fuzz on his legs, my tongue can't wait to taste it. Him. All of him.

"Let's spread these legs, please."

He shimmies his legs open, and his ass shakes and shakes, and fuck, what cosmic favor did I earn in a past life to deserve such a beautiful butt?

"You know you have a juicy ass, right?"

He turns around, eyes wide. "Juicy?"

He laughs, ending with a cough, and I think I've embarrassed him.

"That's a good thing, Coach. Trust me," I say, giving his left cheek a soft slap and then kissing right where my palm landed. "Like a delicious peach."

I grab on to his cheeks and jiggle them, and his ass vibrates in my palms, the movement almost hypnotizing me. I catch a glimpse of his hole in the low light, and I wish I could kneel here forever, playing with his meaty rear.

I pause the assquake and spread him wide. The fuzz on his legs also dots the perimeter, and the soapy smell from his shower infiltrates my nostrils. I strain to catch a bit of his sweat. Maybe next time. My tongue coats my lips like a starving animal eyeing its prey.

"This is what you've been hiding under those track pants," I say.

"Yeah." He's lowered his head between his arms, and I can just make out his mouth.

"You good, Coach?"

He nods rapidly, and I bury my face between his plump, juicy cheeks, diving into his warm hole. He's apprehensive at first, my tongue fighting against his tightness. I keep at it, and I can tell he's trying to let me in, but he needs some guidance.

Pulling back, I lick my lips. "Take a deep breath, Darius."

When I hear the air leaving his lips, I plunge back in, and yup, he's relaxing, opening up, and I can dart deeper.

"Fuck, Harry. Holy. Fuck."

I reach under and grab his cock and stroke it while decorating the inside of his ass with my tongue. Spit and slobber drench my face, and I lose myself in the heat of Darius's opening. He continues to moan and praise me with platitudes, but when I pull his dick back and give it a deep suck, he moves to stand up.

"What?" I ask. "Is something wrong?"

"No, no. It's too intense." He yanks his shoulders back and raises his hands. "I'm close, is all."

"Good."

I move to kiss him but hesitate. He's all over me. Sensing my apprehension, Darius lifts my chin and plants a deep kiss on my lips, unbothered by my face that's drenched in his ass.

I seize his cock, giving it a few long strokes. "Lie on the bed."

He takes my hand and leads me back. With a pillow in hand, I promptly prop it under his butt, providing support and elevating his midsection.

"There we go," I say. "For a coach, you take directions well."

"Please. Direct away."

"Hold your legs up," I say.

Darius hoists his feet up, and my mouth waters at the sight.

"Perfect. Now I'm going to suck you while I play with your ass. Okay?"

"Um, yeah. More than okay."

I rest next to him, taking his cock in one hand, licking and sucking while my index finger teases his taint. When he lifts his hips slightly, I slip my finger inside. All the rimming has him open and ready, and he quickly welcomes my entire digit.

"Fuck, you're horny," I mumble with half his dick in my mouth.

"Harry, I've been horny for you for years."

"Really?" I glance up at him, and he's staring at me doing my best to pleasure him.

"Yes, Harry. My last boyfriend was in college and that was . . . gosh, almost seven years ago now. I've been wild about you from the moment you walked into the teacher's lounge."

Darius's confession leaves me breathless. It's like a switch flips, and my perception of his hostility crumbles, replaced by a new understanding. As he lies with his toes pointing at the headboard and my finger up his ass, I finally see what Darius has been trying to protect all these years. For someone who analyzes complex characters for a living, how did I miss the fact that this guy had a crush on me? I'm like a detective who can't spot a neon sign!

"Want to try another finger?" I ask.

"How about your cock?"

He's stroking me, my dick surging into his grip.

"We're not ready for that," I say. "We don't have condoms. Or lube."

"Maybe next time," he says, panting as my second finger uncorks him from the inside.

"There's going to be a next time?"

"Fuck, I hope so."

He continues stroking me as I resume sucking his cock while I fuck him with my hand, and Darius now leaks so much precum I'm sure I'm hitting his spot. He's close.

"Harry, wait. I'm, oh man. Keep fucking me like that. Wait, harder. Please. Fuck. Harry. Harry. Oh fuck, Harry."

He's coming undone. His hole clenches around my fingers as he fucks my mouth. His eruption is imminent. Darius tangles his fingers in my hair. He's attempting to move me off him. No fucking way. I want to taste all of him.

"Harry, I'm coming," he says, tugging my hair again.

Quickly pulling off, gasping, I plead, "I want your cum, Coach."

And with that, I take him back in, sucking with all my might. It only takes about ten seconds before Darius's balls clench, and hot, thick cum coats the back of my throat like lava as he moans through it. He bucks into my mouth, raising his ass—I think to get me to fuck him harder. I try to push my fingers deeper, despite already reaching their maximum depth.

When the last spasm glides down my throat, with a

heavy sigh, Darius relaxes. "Harry Peterson. What the fuck have you done to me?"

Darius lowers his legs, and he's still while I lick the last drops of cum from the head of his cock.

"Hopefully, whatever it was, it was good?" I ask.

"Not good. Fan-fuckin'-tastic. Now, c'mere."

He takes my hand, guides me up so I'm resting on his chest, and kisses my head.

"I love these damn curls."

My hand smooths over his torso, and I kiss his pec.

"Now, what about you?" he asks.

"Darius, I'm good. I swear. We need to get some sleep."

"Okay, next time. Maybe you can come to the finals with us in Hartford. Coach Applegate isn't going to want to leave all those adorable puppies."

"Hmm. Another hockey game? Yeah, I think I'd like that."

We nestle closer together, and the rhythm of his steady breathing lulls us both into a blissful sleep as I dream about peaches and pucks.

Darius

5

DARIUS

THERE'S an extra pep in my step as I leave my car in the Crossroads Elementary parking lot—not my typical mood on a Monday morning. We won. Okay, technically, it was a tie, but we advanced to the New England finals in Hartford in just under two weeks. As I scan the cars, I spot the navy Corolla with the "Grammar Police" bumper sticker, and my heart trips in my chest.

Harry.

After the game. The night in the hotel room. The one bed I gladly accepted at check-in instead of arguing or asking for a rollaway cot. My fingers wrapped around his blonde curls while I drove my cock between those beautiful lips. The way he devoured my ass like he was starving for it. How he sucked and finger fucked me until I blew my load in his mouth. Fuck.

My dick thickens in my track pants. This isn't how I should be entering school. I pause at the giant metal door, taking a deep breath. Easy does it, boy.

Another inhale, and I enter, waving at Michele, the

secretary who sits behind the window that opens to the entryway. As I head in to check my mailbox, she stops me.

"Coach Hill, I can't believe the boys won! You must be over the moon."

"Tied, Michele, tied."

"But still." Darnelle Stephen emerges from her open office door. "A tie means we advance to the finals."

Leave it to the principal to be Pollyanna.

"This is true. Thanks to the peewee rules," I reply.

"And I heard Mr. Peterson did a bang-up job."

Something becomes lodged in my throat at the mention of Harry's name and the word "job" in the same sentence, and I try and clear it, but I sound like there's a lawn mower stuck in my throat.

"You all right there?" Michele asks as she grabs me a little plastic cup of water from the cooler near the copy machine.

"Yeah, all good. Blow-up job. Bang-up. Bang-up job," I sputter out. "He did great."

The image of Harry's mouth taking me as he moaned flashes in my head, and I shake it away.

"Glad to hear it," Darnelle says. "I had a feeling you two would figure out your differences."

"Did we ever," I mumble.

"Pardon?" Mrs. Stephen cocks an eyebrow, and I force a smile.

Get your damn act together, Darius.

"Nothing. He was great. Harry. Uh, Mr. Peterson. The kids love him."

"Of course they do," Michele says. "Everyone loves

the English teacher. Love poems. Sonnets. *Romeo and Juliet.* What's not to love?"

"Exactly," I say, gulping down the tiny drink she's given me. "Well, I'd better get going. It's dodgeball day. Gotta gather the balls."

The last bit of water gets stuck as I swallow, and a cough escapes. Now, I'm gagging . . . like Harry was Friday night while I fucked his face in the hotel room chair.

"Yeah, um, gotta go." I squash the plastic cup in my hand and toss it into the trash, where it quickly spins around the rim before falling in.

In the hallway, my legs move on autopilot, taking me toward the gym. Teachers walk by. Some are on a mission, carrying papers and supplies, while others walk in pairs, chatting. People wave or say hello, but nobody's really interested in befriending the PE teacher.

I'm lost in the moment, focused on making it to my safety zone, and I don't register when my name echoes in the hallway.

"Coach."

When I blink away my fog, I see him.

Blonde curls.

Brown eyes.

Plump lips.

Harry.

He's with Ms. Wong, the music teacher—Christine, but I always call her Ms. Wong. I call everyone by their honorific. Even the kids. It's just a subtle way to show respect. She's wearing jeans and a colorful sweater with little bees and musical notes on it. My uniform is a tracksuit in two colors—navy and gray. Hers is jeans and corny sweaters.

"Ms. Wong." I nod. "Mr. Peterson."

Harry's eyes flick up to me, then away just as quickly. But in that moment—less than a second, if I were timing it—there's something there.

When I woke up the following day, he was gone. I found him downstairs, sitting with a table of boys avoiding their parents. He was eating a dry English muffin while the kids devoured pancakes, waffles, and enough syrup to drown a moose. We didn't sit together on the bus ride back. When I boarded, he was already sitting near the front, talking to Mr. Winchester, Tommy's dad, about something that sounded vaguely like it had to do with books. Reading. Writing. I don't know, but I headed toward the back and sat with Johnny, still over the moon about his role in securing our spot in the finals.

But that look. I don't care that he wasn't there when I woke up. Or that he chose to spend the bus ride with Tommy's dad. I know there's something there. Here. Between us. Harry's brown eyes lock with mine, and before my brain has a chance to catch up, I blurt out, "Mr. Peterson, can I talk to you for a minute?"

He and Christine pause, and Harry's eyes widen, waiting for me to continue.

"Not here. It's about . . . a student. In my office, if you don't mind."

Christine glances at her watch and says, "You boys go huddle. Or whatever it's called. I need to unpack the new boomwhackers."

"See you at lunch," Harry says to her, but I'm already

headed toward the cafegymatorium, which is being set up for breakfast. The space smells like scrambled eggs and bacon, and I nod at the lunch ladies and head to the back corner where my office is nestled.

As I step inside, I move away from the door to let Harry in. I glide beside him, close the door, secure the lock, then grab his shirt and push him against the metal frame.

My lips are on his, and we're right back in the hotel room. He's inhaling, gasping for air, but also attempting to gulp my face down with it. All the avoidance. The ignored texts. All of it seems to vanish in the seven-by-nine-foot confines of my office.

Harry smells like something clean. Soapy. Laundry maybe? His hands are at my back, clutching me, grabbing, and oh shit, now they're pawing at my ass. With no button, snap, or zipper, I could shimmy out of these track pants easily.

Harry pushes me so I'm against the door now, and he pulls back, peering at me with those deep brown eyes. There's a loose curl covering his right eye, but he's got me pinned, and I don't dare try to move.

With a shake of his head, he silences my question, his mouth covering mine, his tongue pushing past my lips and into my mouth. I'm caught off guard by his sudden move, but the intensity of his kiss quickly consumes me. Our lips dance in a fervent tango, entangled with the yearning desire that's built between us since the first day he walked into Crossroads. Time seems to stand still as our tongues explore, teasing and tasting every inch of each other's mouths. Pinned against the door by Harry, words become unnecessary—the heat of our entwined bodies ignites something profound. Okay, maybe it's just our erections thrashing against each other as the custodian slams tables outside against the floor to prepare for students.

How did I ever doubt his feelings? His lips, they're so damn soft, even as my scruff and his smooth, clean-shaven skin create friction. Harry Peterson might just be the man that ends my dry spell. Well, technically, more of a drought.

There's a nip at my bottom lip, maybe a little harder than he meant, but hey, maybe Harry's caught up in the moment. At this point, he could make me bleed and I wouldn't care. Part of me wonders if we stayed hidden in my office, tucked in the back of the gym forever, if anyone would notice.

"Coach Hill," he says, but he's out of breath, panting. He's sexy as fuck.

"Stop." He pulls back, wiping the saliva from his mouth. "We have to. Stop." Harry points to his mouth, tracing his bottom lip. "This."

"Of course." My track jacket has become all askew from Harry's roughhousing, and I adjust it. "Whatever you say, Harry."

"Also, that. Why are you calling me Harry?"

"Because it's your name."

"In the four years I've been at Crossroads, you've literally never called me Harry. It's always Mr. Peterson. Occasionally 'Teach' or 'Bookworm,' but Harry? Where is this coming from?"

"I thought you might prefer it. Your name. First

name. Harry, um, Peterson, I'll call you whatever you like."

"Coach," he says, walking to the corner of the room, but the baskets of rubber balls block his path.

"Darius," I say. "Or Coach. Coach Hill. Whatever you prefer."

He huffs and then sucks in a deep breath.

"We can't do this. You. Me. What happened at the hotel was a mistake."

And there it is. His words land like a missed shot, a ball bouncing off the rim, leaving the game unfinished.

"Oh."

I don't even realize it comes out of my mouth until it's there, floating between us.

"That's fine. I mean, sure, of course, if that's what you want. Or don't want, I suppose."

I move my hand to the door, preparing to open it for him.

"I just can't. With you. We can't."

I open my mouth to reply, but Harry interrupts me.

"This is what's best."

Harry moves toward the door. Me. But before I open it, letting him out, I ask, "Did I do something wrong?"

He closes his eyes, and I can hear the air escaping his nostrils.

"Never mind," I say and open the door. "See you around, I guess."

And that's it. He walks out of my office, and the silence he leaves behind feels heavier than anything he could have said.

6

DARIUS

I REALLY THOUGHT we had a connection. Sure, physical, but something more. Clearly, I was wrong. I never expected Harry to be the type of guy who hooks up and then ghosts, but I guess I didn't know him as well as I thought. At least we don't have to see each other too often. His class only has PE twice a week, and I can eat lunch in my office to avoid seeing him in the teacher's lounge.

Later that morning, when Lexi gets smashed in the face with a ball, I don't even notice until the screaming reverberates in the gym.

"Coach? Coach?" It's Maynor—Coach Applegate to the kids during practice, but Mr. Applegate during the day when he's a special education aide. He's here to support Lexi and Hugh. Thankfully, he's already kneeling by a very distraught Lexi.

"Sorry, sorry," I stammer to Maynor.

"Fifth graders, water break," I holler. "Then laps." I head over as the rest of the class groans.

"Don't give me attitude," I yell, a little louder than I mean to.

They'll spend most of their time lined up by the fountain, taking long drinks, getting back in line, and barely do a lap around the gym's perimeter by the time we're back to dodgeball, but they complain anyway. They're ten—it's in their DNA.

"What happened?" I ask as I kneel next to Maynor and Lexi.

He's examining her face, and I join him, searching for swelling and/or blood. Lexi's cheeks are red and swollen, but she's also sobbing, so it's hard to discern the culprit.

"She should go to the nurse," I say. "Just to be safe."

He nods, but as he stands, Lexi's crying stops, and she says, "No, I'm okay. I want to keep playing."

Maynor and I exchange a look.

"Why don't you get a drink with the other kids," Maynor says, "and then we'll check in." He glances at me. "We can always stop by Mrs. Lowell's on the way back to class."

Lexi nods and runs over to the line in front of the water fountain. Her sneakers squeak against the shiny gym floor with each quick step, the sound sharp and rhythmic, echoing throughout the otherwise quiet space.

"You okay, Coach?" Maynor rises from the wood floor and wipes his hands on his backside.

"Yeah, fine, just a little tired."

"Sorry again about this weekend. The vet really thought Alice would hold off until after the semis, but, well, Mother Nature has her own schedule."

I nod, and a small smile creeps onto my face. Only Maynor would name his poodle Alice.

"How is she?"

"Surprisingly fine. Six puppies, all doing well. My mother is working from home to keep an eye on them, and so far, besides a few restless nights, everyone's acclimating."

"Glad to hear it." I pull my lips in, watching the first few kids leisurely jog around the black line that paints the perimeter of the gym.

"And you tied. Johnny said it was a miracle on ice, and Mr. Peterson was a great pinch hitter."

Mr. Peterson. Harry. I suck in a gulp of air and slowly push it out of my pursed lips.

"What, was he not? Did something happen?"

Over the past three years, since he started helping me with the hockey team, Maynor and I have become friends. He's invited me over for dinner countless times. Two years ago, when his wife passed, his mother came to support him and never left. She makes the most amazing chicken pot pie. When she tried to set me up with a woman she works with, and I politely declined, she didn't hesitate—without missing a beat, she suggested a male coworker instead.

My eyes close as the chatter of the few kids left in line at the fountain mixes with the squeaks of shoes on the gym floor, making my head spin. I open my mouth, wanting to say something but unsure how to find the words.

"Oh. Listen, Coach," he says, but Hugh, taking his first lap, lingers by the exit, and Maynor needs to attend to him. "On my way back to class, I'm going to drop Lexi at the nurse, take Hugh back to Mrs. Kipp, and come back. You sit. Get a drink. Take some deep breaths. I'll be back in five minutes."

A lump forms in my throat, heavy and tight, as I try to swallow the emotion. On the ice, Maynor may be my assistant, but between being fifteen years older and having way more sense of calm than I could ever muster up, it often feels like he's the one in charge of me.

Maynor wrangles the fifth graders into a line, taking control of the chaos. With the fountain empty, I fill my water bottle, trying to ignore the buzz of energy as he manages them. I've got about fifteen minutes before the next class arrives, so I take a seat on the edge of the bleachers, letting my mind settle for a second. It's quiet for a moment, just the faint echo of sneakers in the hallway and kids' voices fading as Maynor ushers them out. I lean back, running through the situation in my head, trying to catch my breath.

Then Maynor's back, his presence like a shift in the air. He slumps down next to me and takes a breath before glancing at his watch.

"We've got fifteen minutes before your next class starts and my ass needs to be back to Mrs. Kipp. So, Hill, we can sit here in silence, you can hem and haw saying nothing, or you can spill it."

"Twelve minutes." I glance at my watch. "You were lollygagging."

This elicits a smirk from him, but he quickly wipes it away and forces his stern face back.

"Darius."

My first name. He means business.

"Something did happen in Rhode Island."

He raises an eyebrow, waiting for me to continue.

"With Peterson. Mr. Peterson. Harry. The English teacher."

"I'm aware of who he is."

"Turns out there was only one room left at the hotel, and that room only had one bed. And, well . . ."

"Well, what? You and I have shared beds on plenty of away games."

He's really going to make me say it.

"Yeah, but I don't have a massive crush on you, Applegate."

"Thank goodness for that. You're so not my type."

A laugh escapes my lips, grateful he's making light of the situation.

"So you played kissy-face with Mr. Peterson. Good for you." Maynor places his hand on my knee. "Darius, you deserve to be happy."

"That's the thing. I want to be. I've liked Harry for a while now. Years, I guess."

"I figured that's why you're always giving him a hard time."

"You knew?"

"Why else would you tease him so mercilessly?"

"Exactly. See, you get it. But the thing is, even after the . . . kissy-face stuff . . . he doesn't want anything to do with me."

"Did he tell you that?"

"No. Well, sort of. He ignored me the rest of the trip. And this morning, he told me it was all a mistake."

"Oh. I'm sorry, Coach." Maynor pulls his lips in, trying to hide his grin. "Listen, if it helps, one thing I know about courtin' is you can't give up. Did I ever tell you about how I finally nabbed Lucy?"

I shake my head, curious despite myself. Maynor hasn't talked much about Lucy since she passed.

"Well, let me tell you. It wasn't easy. We met in college, back when we were both still figuring out life. I'd seen her around campus, of course—smart, confident, and the kind of woman who walks into a room like she owns it. I'm not gonna lie, I was drawn to her from the first moment I saw her." He chuckles, shaking his head as if the memory still amuses him.

"But Lucy? She wasn't interested in me at all. Not at first. She had this whole 'I'm focused on my future' vibe, and I was just some guy on the hockey team who made terrible jokes and had no clue how to talk to women. I tried everything—inviting her to study groups, sitting near her in the dining hall, but she barely gave me the time of day." He pauses, a smirk creeping up his face. "I've never seen someone dodge a guy's advances so smoothly. It was like watching someone avoid a puddle— she just glided right around me."

I laugh softly, trying to picture it.

"But you didn't give up, did you?" I ask.

"Nope," he says, shaking his head again, more serious now. "I was persistent. I kept showing up, kept being myself, even when it felt like she didn't notice. And eventually, after months of me just being around—after all those terrible dates I set up that ended in 'Let's just be friends,' she finally saw something in me. Maybe she saw the effort I was putting in, maybe she saw I wasn't going anywhere, but one night, after a late study session, she asked me to grab a coffee. Just the two of us."

"And that was it?" I ask, surprised at how simple it sounds.

"Yeah," he nods, looking almost nostalgic. "It's funny how that works. Sometimes you don't know when the moment's going to hit, but when it does, everything falls into place. It wasn't some grand gesture. It was just me being there. And the next thing I knew, we were together."

I can see the heartache in his eyes, and I reach over and squeeze his shoulder. "You two had something special."

He nods, taking a deep inhale.

"I think I get what you're saying," I say. "Keep showing up?"

Maynor grins, his usual easy confidence back. "Exactly. You keep showing up, Coach. You never know when it'll click."

"All right, Applegate," I say, squeezing his shoulder. "I need to get the balls reset."

"And I need to get back to class. Remember, keep showing up."

With that, I turn and head toward my office, feeling a bit lighter than before. Maybe there's more to this whole "showing up" thing than I realized. Thoughts of how to reach Harry and show him my resolve chase each other through my mind. I know there's something between us, and I'm not giving up.

7

DARIUS

I'M STANDING by the hallway entrance to the gym when Harry walks up with his class. Fifth graders have PE twice a week, and regardless of how much he'd like to avoid me, we have to see each other at least these few moments when he drops them off and picks them up.

But something's off with Harry. He's usually calm and collected, especially with his students. But not today. I sense it immediately—the tension in his shoulders, the tightness around his eyes as he hurries Penny at the front of the line into the gym.

He checks his watch as the class files in, heading to the center circle and sitting. This is their third year at Crossroads, and they know what I expect.

When the last few in line cross the doorway, I call to them, "Two minutes of deep breathing. Center yourselves for dodgeball."

"Hey, you okay?" I ask Harry, my voice low, but not so much that it feels like an interrogation.

Harry exhales, long and loud. "Yeah, I'm fine. Just

forgot my lunch," he mutters, and I can tell by the way his jaw clenches that it's more than just a minor inconvenience.

"Forgot your lunch?" I repeat, raising an eyebrow. Harry doesn't seem like the type of guy who forgets anything. "What happened?"

He shrugs, rubbing the back of his neck. "Being away the first part of the weekend . . ." He shoots me a look, not having to say more about him unexpectedly chaperoning. "I was catching up on planning yesterday but didn't get a chance to hit the store. And I need to eat during my prep this afternoon because I have lunch duty today."

I know exactly what he means. Lunch duty is a commitment. Chattering kids and scraping chairs blend into one long, noisy symphony. You can't just shove a sandwich in your face and call it a day. And anyway, it sounds like Harry doesn't have a sandwich to shove.

I feel a grin tug at my mouth. "Listen, I've got time at lunch. I know a little sandwich shop just off Cumberland. It's tucked back between some houses. They make the best melts. Tuna melt. Turkey melt. Veggie melt, if that's your jam. I can run and grab something for you. What do you want?"

"No, no, it's fine. I've got some crackers in the classroom for the kids who forget snacks."

My heart sinks because I know the drill. Kids forget, or worse, their families don't have the resources, and the school doesn't step up to help. Who picks up the slack from their own underfunded pockets? Teachers.

"Worst-case scenario," he says with a groan. "I can always just grab . . ." He gulps. "School lunch." His tone drips with disdain as he says it, and I can't say I blame him.

"Don't torture yourself," I say. "It's hot dogs and beans today."

That seems to do it. His face twists like he's just smelled something foul. He sighs, giving in. "Fine. I'll take you up on your offer. But I'm not picky. Anything's fine."

He reaches for his wallet, but I stop him.

"My treat." I give him a quick nod and head over to the students before he can protest or change his mind.

Class is uneventful. Johnny wins the first round and, riding high from his assist at the big game, there's a shift in the way the other students are treating him. It's heart-warming to watch kids discover their passions and talents.

When Harry picks them up, I've already got my track jacket on and my car keys in my pocket. I could walk to Sammy's Sammies but want to get there and back as quickly as possible. Because fourth grade has lunch during this period, there's no class in the gym, so I have my prep period.

When I return, walking through the corridor with the sandwich shop bag, it feels like I'm carrying the weight of the entire planning period in my hand. I head to Harry's classroom, the faint sounds of students singing about Jimmy cracking corn drifting into the hallway as I pass Christine's room. Good, he's alone.

I knock once, then open the door.

"Lunchtime," I say, setting the bag on his desk. He looks up, and for a moment, that weight on his face seems to ease. He glances at the bag like it's a small miracle.

"You're a lifesaver," he mutters, tearing open the bag. He pulls out two wrapped sandwiches—one marked with a V and the other a T.

"Veggie and tuna melts. You choose because I'll smash either."

It registers on his face. One is for me. I pull a chair out at the small kidney-shaped table near his desk. I've seen teachers pull small groups at these, and I figure it'll make a fine place to eat.

"Don't worry, I'll clean the table after."

Harry lets out a small sigh, then presses his lips in. "Why don't we split them?" He stands and walks over to the chair in the middle, behind the table. "This way I can try both."

A foolish smile forms on my face. He's relenting. At least for lunch.

Harry opens the sandwiches, using the brown bag as a plate. He takes half of each for himself, then slides the other combined sandwich over to me on the paper they were wrapped in. My mind races, thinking of the next right thing to say, but comes up completely empty. For now, we're here, eating our sandwiches, and for a minute, it's just us. Quiet—the weight of the day paused.

"Damn, this is good." His mouth is full, but he covers it with the sandwich.

He's started with the veggie, just some random vegetables slathered in smoked gouda. A thin, almost invisible string of melted cheese stretches from his bottom lip when he puts the sandwich down. I nod in his general direction and hand him a napkin from the pile between us, which he places on his lap.

"No, Harry, you've got a little . . ." I reach over, swiping at the cheese and wiping it on my napkin.

"Thanks," he says.

"They use a ton of cheese," I reply. "That's what makes it so tasty."

"No, I meant for this. Lunch. Going to get it. You didn't have to do that." He picks the tuna half up. "How much do I owe you? I don't have any cash, but I can send you money. Or get cash after school?"

"I told you, Harry. It's on me. It's my pleasure. Truly."

His eyes flit up at me, and then he sinks into the sandwich. "Okay, how did I not know about this place? Sammy's Sammies?"

"Teachers don't have time to go out at lunch. With two consecutive lunch periods in the cafeteria, I get a double prep. And it's always splat in the middle of the day. Sometimes, I walk around. You find things."

"And sometimes you hang out in the teacher's lounge, making my life miserable."

"Harry, I thought we went over this. When a boy teases someone . . ."

"Yeah, yeah, I remember."

"Is that what this is all about? Are you mad because I razzed you for . . ."

"Years."

"Well, let me officially apologize." I set my veggie melt down. "Harry Peterson, I'm sorry I teased you. I was an immature ass who didn't know how to express his feelings, so instead I taunted you."

I take a deep breath. Now's not the time to hold back.

"It's like I'm stuck between two worlds. Most people assume I'm straight—probably because of all the sports."

"And the hat."

"Yeah, that doesn't help." I tug on the brim. "But I'm not. And whenever I try to meet guys at clubs or bars, they don't really get me either—because of, well . . . the sports."

"Don't forget the hat." A hint of a smile tugs at his lips.

"Do you really hate it that much?"

"No. It's kind of cute, actually."

My body relaxes into the chair. "And you, Harry . . . you're so damn smart. Handsome. You're into books and theater and all this stuff I know nothing about. And even though you made my insides turn to mush, I was sure someone like you would never give someone like me the time of day."

"So you teased me."

"If I could take it all back, I would. I should've just told you how I felt from the start."

Harry chews on my apology—and his lunch.

"Hey, I've got an idea," I say as I stand.

"That sounds dangerous."

"No, listen. I'm going to walk out of the room and come back in, and we'll pretend it's your first day here at Crossroads."

Before he can object, I'm out the door. With a quick

shake of my shoulders, I walk back in, determined to make this right.

"Hey, there, I'm Darius Hill—PE teacher and peewee hockey coach. What's your name?"

Harry looks at me like I have ten heads.

"Harry Peterson," I say. "Nice to meet you." I retake my seat, leaving my half-eaten sandwich. "I know you're new here. Maybe we could grab coffee sometime? Let me give you my number." I grab a pad of sticky notes and a pencil from the little caddy in the middle of the table and jot my cell down. "Here, text me if you have questions about school or whatever. Or call. Welcome to Crossroads!"

Harry dips his chin as his eyebrows rise. He's not buying it.

"Oh, and I'm gay. Yeah, I know, never would've guessed it from the tracksuit and intense interest in sports. And the hat. But I am. Totally gay. Gay, gay, gay. If you don't believe me, I could dig up a few numbers of guys who could vouch for me."

Because I'm staring at his face, I notice the first signs of Harry's lips turning up. Nothing spurs me on like a cute guy smiling.

"Let's see, Doug was my boyfriend in college. We haven't talked in years, but I think I could message him online. And I hooked up with some stranger about five years ago during Pride in Ogunquit. Rick. Richard. Dick? Well, yeah, there was definitely dick. But I can't be sure of his name. I could hire a skywriter and try to track him down."

Harry's full-on laughing now. His lunch rests beside

mine, and his beautiful blonde curls bounce as his body shakes with laughter.

"Okay, okay, enough," he manages through chuckling, his laugh warm and easy.

It makes me want to gather him up next to me on a blanket under the stars.

"Anyway, I'm sorry." My heart races, but I puff my chest out, determined to keep eye contact. "For being a dick. For so long."

Harry stares at me for a moment. His eyes scan my face, searching.

"I'm partial to long dicks," he says.

"Good one," I say.

The desire to spend more time with Harry consumes me like a relentless player chasing the winning shot at the buzzer.

"You didn't get to experience the ice in Warwick. Let me take you."

His face drops, and he picks up his sandwich. "Darius, I don't do sports. You know this."

"Skating isn't sports. We're not playing hockey or doing double axels. Just skating. It's barely cardio." I widen my eyes and give him my best pleading face. "Come on, Peterson. It'll be fun. I promise."

"That's what I'm afraid of."

"You'll want to be comfortable on the ice before we head to Hartford next week."

I wiggle my eyebrows at him.

"Who said anything about me going to the finals?"

"Coach Applegate has a litter of puppies to look after. And the team loves you. Come on, Harry."

He swipes the sticky notes and pen from the table, jots something, and slides it over.

"My address. Tomorrow night. Pick me up at six."

A victorious grin plasters across my face.

"But if I fall, I'm blaming you."

I chuckle. "Deal."

I carefully tuck Harry's address into my pocket. As he picks up his sandwich again, I catch the slightest hint of another smile tugging at the corner of his mouth.

He's probably not looking forward to it, but deep down, I know he's going to have a blast.

"I'll pick you up tomorrow at six, Peterson," I repeat with a wink.

He rolls his eyes but doesn't argue. It's happening. We're going on a skating date.

8

DARIUS

IT TAKES extra energy to focus on the tasks at hand all day. When Rebecca uses three hula hoops to be funny, I don't even notice until the entire class bursts into laughter. I'm so fucking excited about seeing Harry and taking him on an actual date. I've been waiting years for this moment, and I don't want to screw it up.

I'm in front of Harry's building ten minutes early in my old green Saab 900. I know it's not the most glamorous ride, but I've had it since college, and it's got this charm. It's a classic. Fuck, it's even a standard. It makes a weird sound when I brake, but they're brand new, so I do my best to ignore it.

I don't want to seem too eager, so I check the scores on my phone. I won't text Harry and tell him I'm here for at least five minutes. Maynor couldn't have been more right. Showing up works. Getting Harry lunch felt like such a small gesture, yet it made me feel fantastic. I thought I was doing him this huge favor, but in reality, I benefited from the good vibes it brought me.

I put my phone down and close my eyes, and Harry's face floats into my mind—his beautiful brown eyes. Those soft sandy-blond curls. And his lips. The way they felt on mine. For as long as I can remember, my lips had been searching for something. And then, with Harry's kiss, they finally felt complete.

My heart races, thinking about what this night means. I want that feeling again. Yeah, the sex was mind-blowing, but it's not even that. I want his lips on mine. To hold him in my arms. To listen to him breathe while he sleeps.

I'm taken out of my Harry trance by a tapping on the passenger window. It's him. Crap.

I unlock the door, and he's sitting next to me, lips pulled into a careful smile.

"Wait, Harry, no. I was going to text you." I'm shaking my head, frustrated I'm already fucking this up. "At least get the car door for you. Can you get out and let me do that?"

He tilts his head and scrunches his eyebrows together. Damn, he's cute.

"Please," I say.

"Fine."

We both exit the car, and I jog around and place my hand on the handle while Harry stands, waiting.

"Harry," I say, opening the door.

But he doesn't get in.

"Is something wrong?" I ask.

He shakes his head. "No, but you don't have to do all this."

"I know, but I want to."

Harry moves to sit but pauses when his face comes close to mine, giving me the smallest, barely there kiss on the cheek.

Hot damn.

The warmth of his lips lingers on my skin, sending a flutter of surprise through me. He pulls back just slightly, his gaze softening as he catches my eye, a quiet smile playing at the corners of his mouth. The air between us is charged, and my heart beats a little faster, unsure of what this simple gesture means but grateful for it all the same.

He's sitting. In the car. Waiting. And I'm standing by the door like I've just seen a flying saucer land.

"Coming, right there, Harry. Um, Peterson."

I dash around to the driver's side, sit, and pull the door shut. When I turn to grab the seat belt, Harry's there, his handsome face smiling at me with those fucking lips.

"Slow down, Coach." He leans over and takes my jaw in his hands. "Relax."

And then he gently places his lips on mine. In that moment, a wave of warmth washes over me as my body melts into his touch, surrendering completely to the sensation of Harry Peterson's kiss. Every nerve in my body ignites, and I lose myself in the sweet intimacy of our connection. Cars drive by. Birds sing. The earth continues to spin on its axis. But inside my old Saab, it all seems to blur as Harry's tongue dances inside my mouth.

He grabs my jacket, pulling me closer, and the way he's kissing me, the way my cock reacts, I'm not sure how I'm going to get through what I've planned for the rest of the night.

He pulls back, and before my brain catches up to what's happening, I say, "Are you hungry?"

Harry's eyes widen, and I blurt out, "For dinner. I know this cozy Italian place. Rudy's. Best damn chicken parm I've ever had. It'll make your toes tingle. Whaddya say?"

He nods, and his tongue traces over his lips. Maybe he really loves chicken parm?

"Darius, I know this is technically our first date, but I figured after the night in Rhode Island, instead of waiting all night and wondering if there'd be a kiss, we could start with it."

"No complaints from me."

He beckons me back over to his side with a finger, and when I lean his way, he kisses me again. Short and sweet, but right on the lips.

"Peterson, you're going to spoil me with all this kissing."

And how does he reply? By doing it again. My heart ramps up again from his touch, and the smile on my face could rival the fireworks on the Fourth of July.

"I mean, if that's all it takes," he says. "You're an easy date."

I drive off and am barely at the end of his block when Harry takes my hand and holds it on top of the center console. I suppose after the night in the hotel, kissing and holding hands might be considered a step backward, but I couldn't be happier about it.

When we walk into Rudy's, the look on Harry's face is a mix of curiosity and slight hesitation. The restaurant is small, almost snug in its tightness, with only a handful of tables scattered across the space. Each one is tucked into the corners, giving the place an intimate, almost homey feel. The walls are painted in soft, warm tones, and old wooden beams run across the ceiling, adding character to the building. The smell of Italian food lingers in the air, comforting and inviting.

From the outside, it's almost indistinguishable from one of the houses in the neighborhood, with its simple, unassuming facade—just a small sign hanging above the door that reads "Rudy's" in faded letters. The windows are small and framed with delicate curtains, offering a glimpse inside but not enough to reveal its full charm. It's the kind of spot you might walk right by if you didn't know it was there, but once you step inside, it's clear that Rudy's is a hidden gem, a place where the noise of the world fades and you're enveloped in the warmth of good food and quiet conversation.

"Coach! Coach!" It's Rudy, who somehow hosts, waits on all the tables, and runs the kitchen.

He hugs me, and I'm surrounded by the sweet smell of cooked onions and garlic.

"How are the Sharks? Making lots of waves?"

"We actually made the finals. We're headed to Hartford next weekend."

"Congratulations! Those kids are lucky to have you. And who is this?" Rudy raises an eyebrow and extends his hand to Harry.

"I'm Harry Peterson. I teach English at Crossroads with Darius."

Rudy cocks his head, studying Harry, then his eyes move to me, a glint of recognition flickering in them. I played hockey with his son, Marco, throughout under-grad, and he knows I'm gay. Marco and I shared an apartment during our senior year. He had a girlfriend, and I was with Doug. And while I'm not sure if Marco ever said anything directly, I'm sure his father must have caught on. Rudy's gaze lingers, but there's no judgment, just an understanding that doesn't need words.

Rudy seats us at the best table—the one closest to the kitchen—and heads off to another table. It's tucked away in a corner, and even though two other couples are here, it feels like we have the whole place to ourselves.

"I'm not sure if you like chicken parm, but seriously, Rudy's will change your life."

"Transformative chicken Parmesan. I'm intrigued."

I don't want to push Harry too hard, but the need to apologize hovers over me like a ghost.

"Look, about all the stuff I said," I start, my voice careful. "The way I treated you. Harry, I meant it when I said I was sorry. But . . . if I'm honest . . .that guy? The one who said all that crap? That was me. It's just—" I hesitate, thinking it over. "I guess I didn't know how else to get your attention. But I don't want to be that guy anymore."

Harry looks up from his plate, his gaze deadpan. "You mean the one with his dick down my throat?"

I almost choke on the fresh bread Rudy placed on the table. I swallow hard, twice, just to make sure I'm not going to embarrass myself. I wasn't expecting that. From him. But the way he said it—so casual, so matter-of-fact—it surprised me. He didn't flinch or back away. Just tossed it out there like it was no big deal to say it in the middle of Rudy's.

I wipe my mouth, trying to recover. "Uh, yeah, I mean, I do want to be that guy. I mean the one with his . . . The one I was in the hotel room. Not before."

He's got me all flustered. My thoughts jumble, and I can hardly focus. It's as if he has this incredible power over me that leaves me breathless and anxious, struggling to find my words. Every little interaction sends my heart racing and makes me second-guess myself. It's both exciting and overwhelming.

We sit for a moment, the silence uncomfortable now. Thankfully, Rudy comes with his little notepad and pen to take our order.

With a quick nod, Harry orders first. "I'll take the chicken Parmesan. I've heard it's spectacular." He winks at me, and my stomach does a flip. "And can I get a little side salad?"

"Of course," Rudy replies. "All our meals come with bread, salad, and a side of pasta. Would you like spaghetti, linguini, or fusilli?"

"Oh, I'll have the linguini."

"Perfect. And for you, Coach?"

"I'll have the same."

"Amazing. Would you like some wine?"

"None for me," I say.

"I'll have a glass of merlot." Harry glances at me, and I nod as Rudy scribbles on his notepad and zooms back to the kitchen.

Once Harry has his wine, talking seems easier for him. I'd love a glass, but I'm driving—and Harry's already got me distracted. Rudy brings the food out, and as I hoped, Harry's enthralled.

"Oh, my gosh. You weren't kidding, Darius. This is amazing."

"Rudy doesn't mess around. I've been eating here since college. Well, eating his food. In college, it was more of Rudy bringing takeout to our dumpy apartment situation."

"Wait, so you dated his son?"

"Oh gosh, no, Marco and I were roommates. As in, actual roommates. He had a girlfriend. We weren't in some fantasy hockey world where straight dudes suddenly want to bang their teammates. We were friends. And Rudy brought us Sunday dinner most weeks."

"Okay, not Rudy's son, but your last boyfriend was in college?"

"Yes, Doug. We dated for almost a year, which at the time felt like an eternity. Now I realize how short that really was."

"And nobody since?"

"Dating? Nope. I've hooked up with a few guys. Last time was about three years ago. I was feeling lonely and downloaded one of those apps. You know, where you're matched with guys based on your location. It was fine. I mean, it did the trick, but the whole thing felt off for me. The guy was friendly enough, but he had no interest in staying when it was over. No talking. No cuddling. Nothing like . . ."

"Rhode Island." Harry leans over his plate, offering a genuine smile that makes my pulse race.

"Listen, Harry, when you walked into the teacher's lounge four years ago, you immediately grabbed my attention. And yeah, teasing you so hard makes me an immature goofball, but I only did it because I had such a major crush on you."

"Yeah, I've figured that out."

"So," I said, leaning in a little, "about the next part of the night—"

Harry raises an eyebrow, looking skeptical. "Next part? Skating?"

I nodded. "Yeah, I've got a plan. Thought we could keep this going."

He leans back in his chair, glancing at his watch. "Um . . . it's a school night."

I grin. "Oh, don't worry, Cinderella. I'll have you home before you turn into a pumpkin."

He rolls his eyes, then smirks. "Is that the extent of your literary knowledge? A fairy tale that was made into a Disney film?"

"Hey, those mice are hella cute."

Harry's eyes widen, and we both laugh. He's mocking me, but in that way that makes my insides all gooey. We're in sync now, the teasing flowing both ways. And for the first time tonight, I can tell he's all in. That wall he'd been keeping up? It's crumbling.

9

DARIUS

THE COLD AIR hits me as I step out of the car, biting at my skin. It's mid-March, but winter's not ready to let go yet—there's still a thick blanket of snow on the ground, and the icy wind cuts through my jacket like it's got a personal vendetta against me. The outdoor rink run by the parks division isn't too crowded, though, which I guess makes sense for a Thursday night. A few people glide along the edges, but it's mostly empty.

I glance over at Harry, who's still in the passenger seat, looking like he'd rather be anywhere else but at a skating rink. We had such a delightful time at Rudy's, and I'm determined to carry that over here.

He looks at me with wide eyes. "You know I don't skate, right?" he asks, his voice tinged with uncertainty. "As in, I don't skate because I don't know how."

I laugh, shaking my head. "Yeah, I know. But I do. I'm gonna teach you."

He looks less than convinced but nods, grabbing his

jacket and stepping out into the chilly night. I pop open the trunk, the freezing air making my breath puff out in little clouds. Inside, there are two pairs of skates—one that I've had for years and one that's a bit newer. I hold them up, giving them a quick once-over.

"Think these'll fit?" I ask, tossing them over to him. "I wasn't sure about your shoe size, but based on . . . Warwick, I guessed we're almost the same size."

He misses them, the poor skates landing on the ground with a clank.

"I told you. Zero athletic ability." He picks them up, looks them over, and then glances at his shoes. "Were you checking out my feet in Rhode Island?"

"Yes, Harry. I was checking out every inch of you."

My tone may be sarcastic, but indeed I was.

"Well, let's see if they fit." He scrubs his hands over his face and sighs, but he doesn't back out.

We sit on one of the benches around the rink's perimeter. I take a deep breath, excited despite the cold, and start lacing up my skates. A small part of me hopes Harry falls a hundred times tonight—he'll need catching.

"So?" I ask, watching him adjusting his foot inside the first skate.

"Like a glove."

He smiles up at me, and damn if my heart doesn't melt.

Turns out we do wear almost the same size shoe. I'm taking that as another sign from the universe about us. As we head toward the rink, Harry has that baby-deer-learning-to-walk vibe as he tries to balance on the skates. I can't wipe the giant grin off my face as I watch him wobble. He's so damn cute it hurts.

I can't think of a more fun activity for an actual first date with Harry Peterson than skating. A lightness swarms my chest when Harry staggers and grabs onto my arm for balance. I've taught hundreds of kids to skate, so I'm fairly confident I can get him up and going. I can already imagine his expression when he gets it—shaky at first and then finally confident. There's something about skating together that feels . . . almost perfect.

"All right," I say, turning back to him as we get to the edge of the rink. "First things first, use your arms for balance. Then just let yourself glide. No sudden movements, okay? You've gotta trust the ice."

Harry raises an eyebrow. "Trust the ice? I barely trust myself."

"Well," I grin, offering him my hand, "that's why I'm here. You stay next to me, all right? I'll catch you if you fall."

He hesitates for a second then grabs my hand. His grip's a little tense, but that's fine. I'm used to teaching children who have surprisingly powerful grips. I guide him out onto the ice, my skates cutting through the surface with ease. Harry's stiff, like he's afraid of toppling already, and I can't help but chuckle as he teeters along behind me.

"Come on," I tease, slowing down so he can catch up. "You've got this. It's just like walking but on ice."

He shoots me a look, clearly not convinced. "If walking was this hard, I'd never leave my house."

I laugh again, shaking my head. "God, you're adorable."

He squeezes my hand, and I keep prodding him along. "You're doing fine. Just try to glide, no need to rush. Think of it as pushing off with each step."

Eventually, after a few more tries, he starts to get the hang of it. His legs aren't shaking as much, and he's leaning into it a little more.

Then, just as he's finding a rhythm, his face softening and smile creeping in, he sways, arms out, and tumbles backward. But I'm right there to grab him, jutting my arms under his as I take on the entirety of his weight.

"See?" I say, smiling over him. "Told you I'd catch you."

Harry rolls his eyes but grins back. "Yeah, yeah. You're my hero. Just . . . don't expect me to be as good as you any time soon."

"Stop being so charming, Harry."

He smirks, but keeping a hold of my hand, he tries again.

We keep going like that—him unsteady, me teasing him a little, but all in good fun. And by the time the night starts winding down, I can tell he's actually enjoying himself. He might not admit it yet, but I can see it in the way his smile's a little brighter, how he's becoming more confident on the ice.

"This was a good idea," he says as we take a break, sitting on the side of the rink, our skates off and resting against the snowbanks.

I grin. "Yeah, I figured it'd be fun. You know, a little

adventure in the middle of a cold, boring week. Plus, this will earn you points with the Sharks."

"Not if they see how terrible I am." He glances over at me, his expression soft.

As if Mother Nature wants to add a little magic to our evening, a soft snowfall begins to float around us.

"I had a good time, Darius. Even if I'm pretty sure I'll be sore tomorrow."

"That's the price of learning," I say, nudging him with my shoulder. "But hey, you did great. You'll be an expert in no time."

"Yeah, right." He laughs.

And in this moment, with the snow gently falling around us and the rink quiet except for our laughter, I know in my heart, this is one of those nights that's gonna stick with me for a while.

THE ENGINE'S hum fills the silence between us. Streetlights blur past as I drive, the steady rhythm of the tires on the road almost too soothing, like it's trying to lull me into forgetting what's on my mind. Harry's sitting right next to me, quiet for once, his eyes focused outside. I keep stealing glances at him, wondering if he feels the same tension that's been building since we left the rink.

God, I keep thinking about last weekend—how close we were, the way he looked at me just before we pulled away. It's like that moment is still alive between us, in the way he's sitting next to me now, his hand close enough for me to touch.

We're almost at his place, and I lick my lips to moisten my dry mouth with little success. I grab for the mints in the center console, and the rattling in the plastic container pulls Harry's focus.

"Mint?"

He raises his eyebrows, and fuck, I wasn't trying to be presumptuous.

"Sure." He holds his hand out, and I shake three into his palm.

After popping a few in my mouth, the coolness helping me produce some saliva, my mind races as we approach his apartment. What if he invites me up? It's late, and we have school tomorrow, but maybe . . . between dinner and skating, the way I caught him and he held my hand . . . maybe he wants to keep the night going, right? I can't shake the thought, the way his hand rests casually on the seat, just inches away from mine. Maybe we could talk some more. Maybe he'd want me to stay over.

Or maybe I'm overthinking it.

I glance at him, and he catches my eye, giving me that half smile that's so damn distracting. He leans back in the seat, stretching out a little, and I wonder if he's thinking the same things.

"Hey," I say, voice a little rougher than I mean. "I had a lot of fun. It was a good night, don't you think?"

He nods, his lips curling into a small smile. "Yeah. It really was."

The words feel loaded, like something unspoken hangs between us, something too delicate to name. I shift my gaze back to the road, focusing on the lights ahead, my mind still reeling.

I pull up to his place, the soft glow of his building lighting up the curb, and I let out a breath I didn't realize I was holding.

Harry unbuckles his seatbelt slowly, his hand hovering for just a second over the door handle. The weight of the moment looms over me, and Maynor's voice echoes in my head: keep showing up.

He looks over at me again, and this time, his smile's a little softer.

"I . . . I should probably head in," he says, his voice quieter now. "It's late."

I nod, trying to keep my cool, though my mind's racing. "Sure. We both have to get up early tomorrow."

"Yes, but it's not that."

There's a fluttering in my stomach, hoping I haven't messed up . . . again.

"Tonight was really . . . special, you know?" He takes my hand, removes my glove, and laces his fingers with mine.

My damn heart nearly leaps out of my chest.

"And even though . . ."

"Rhode Island," I say.

"Exactly. Let's just enjoy the night for what it was."

"And what's that, Harry?"

"A wonderful first date."

For a moment, I think he's going to say more. The thought is there, just on the edge of everything, but instead, he looks at me like he's trying to say goodbye without actually saying the words.

I lean toward him because I don't know how to thank him. We're so close, but I don't want to make the wrong move.

"Would it be okay if I gave you a kiss goodnight?"

"Such a gentleman," he says. "I'd like that."

His eyes flicker down to my mouth, and I get that weird tunnel-vision thing for just a second, like when I've skated too hard without eating enough beforehand. Then, without thinking, I close the space between us.

His kiss is soft at first, tentative. Even though it's not our first kiss, it's our first kiss after our first date. A soft moan escapes my lips because, after all this time, I've finally been on an actual date with Harry Peterson.

And then, maybe spurred on by the noises I can't seem to stop, it deepens, and I forget about everything except the feel of his lips on mine, the warmth of his breath against my cheek. His tongue dances with mine, and at some point, he nibbles my upper lip. It hurts, but in a way that feels amazing.

"Fuck, Peterson."

He's back, kissing, biting, licking the inside of my mouth, and I'm so grateful I sucked on those mints. For a moment, I consider moving my hands from his chest to his groin, but then I remember what he said about it being the perfect night and wanting to preserve that memory as it is, so I don't.

When we pull apart, there's nothing left to say, just the quiet of the night outside my Saab.

He looks at me, his eyes soft and full of something I can't quite name.

"Goodnight, Darius," he says, a little breathless.

Leaning over, Harry plants the softest, sweetest kiss on my lips. Fuck, I could get used to this.

"See you in the morning." He runs his thumb down my jawline and then moves to open the door.

I nod, my hand resting on the gearshift, as I try to recover from kissing him. "Good night, Harry."

Harry

10

HARRY

"HE BROUGHT SKATES FOR YOU?"

"He did. It was . . . sweet."

Christine and I may have finished with this year's musical, but we typically begin planning for next year immediately after. It gives us an excuse to eat lunch in one of our rooms a couple days a week and talk about topics we typically wouldn't in the teacher's lounge. Today, we're in my classroom, and she's brought a tub of her homemade coconut chocolate chip cookies.

"Honestly, Harry. You and Coach Hill hooking up was not on my bingo card."

Christine's black hair is pulled up into a high pony-tail. I'm not entirely sure how it stays up, but there's always at least one pencil sticking out of it, sometimes two.

"To be fair, it wasn't on mine either." I take a bite of the turkey sandwich I made this morning and wish it was a melt from Sammy's.

"He brought me lunch." I scoot back from the kidney-shaped table and cross my legs.

"Darius Hill made that pathetic dry-ass turkey sandwich for you?" Her hair shakes in perpetual motion as she tilts her head.

"No, no. I made this. He saved the day last week when I forgot my lunch. I didn't have time to shop over the weekend."

"Because you were exhausted from your sexy hotel romp with the hot, awful, but maybe not-so-awful-anymore PE teacher-slash-hockey coach."

"Exactly." I abandon my sandwich for the bag of salt and vinegar chips. "And the jury's still out. I'm proceeding with extreme caution."

"But, you're proceeding."

"He brought me skates."

"It's like a bad cable TV romantic comedy." She pokes at her salad, presumably hoping for it to turn into something other than salad. "I wish Landon would take me skating. Or to dinner. Or to a crappy hotel with the peewee hockey team so we could have amazing hotel sex."

"Well, Landon's straight. Straight guys rarely do romantic stuff."

"Yes, but until very recently, we thought Darius was straight."

"True. But he's not." I shrug at the realization we were both completely wrong about him. "Most definitely not."

My eyebrows raise as I crunch on another chip. Four years. That's a long time to think something about someone and find out you're completely wrong. I don't regret what happened in Rhode Island. It was fun. And hot. I'm not one to lust after straight guys, so I never really considered Darius. Plus, he teased me in that way that reminded me way too much of the boys in middle school. And then, of course, the sports. The way my father and brothers always were playing sports or talking about sports or planning to attend sports. Darius is the PE teacher. Hockey coach. My complete lack of hand-eye coordination has instilled in me a lifelong fear of anything related to sports. And guys don't come much sportier than Darius.

I shake my head, trying to push away the uncertainty. He apologized. Brought me lunch. Sat with me. Bought me dinner. Had skates for me. Caught me when I fell. And the kissing. That wasn't *first date, let's see how the chemistry is* kissing. That was soul-changing, insides-on-fire kissing. It's like a switch flipped in that hotel room, and Darius turned into someone else. Someone who not only likes me but treats me like a prince.

But has the man he was for all those years really disappeared? Or has he simply stopped pretending? Maybe he hasn't changed at all—maybe this is who he's been the whole time, just hidden behind a carefully constructed mask. Now, the mask has slipped, and what we're seeing isn't a transformation but a revelation. Perhaps the truth was always there, lurking in the shadows, waiting for the moment he no longer felt the need to hide it—in bed with me.

"*Damn Yankees*," Christine says.

"Excuse me? You know I don't do sports."

"Besides the hockey coach?" She wiggles her eyebrows. "I'm talking about the show. For next year. With you connecting with the boys on the hockey team—and their coach—in a new way, I'm thinking we can finally pull off a show with so many male parts. Plus, it's sports-adjacent, and now we can ask Darius to consult. I'm sure he'd be happy to spend extra time with you."

A noise comes out of me I'm not familiar with. Something between a groan and grumble.

"What?" Christine has given up on her salad and moved onto the tupperware of cookies she's baked for us. "Hearing 'Whatever Lola Wants, Lola Gets' belted in the cafegymatorium doesn't interest you?"

"Christine Wong, you're not playing Lola."

"I know!" Cookie crumbs fall onto the table as she protests. "But it would be such campy fun for one of the girls."

I take a cookie. "Or boys. Remember, Apollo played Ursula. And he nailed it."

"Whoever. I just love that show. We need more sports representation on the stage."

"Damn, Christine. These are your best yet." I do my best to talk with a full mouth. "Crisp on the outside and gooey in the middle."

"It's the coconut," she says, mouth full, not that either of us cares. "I use organic, too. None of that hydrolyzed chemical stuff. That's the secret."

"I've never had anything so scrumptious in my mouth." I cover my lips, attempting to have a modicum of decorum. "Heavenly."

"What's so heavenly in your mouth?" A voice comes from the cracked door.

We both turn toward the culprit. Darius.

"My cookies," Christine says, standing and offering him the container. "Want one?"

"I do love cookies." Darius closes the classroom door, takes a treat, and then, without batting an eye, sits in the chair closest to me.

The chair I keep for kids who need to sit next to me because they're distracting the class and themselves and unable to do any independent work without being right next to the teacher.

And then, without saying another word, he leans over and kisses my cheek.

"Harry."

The word comes out of his mouth softer than I expect, and I'm caught somewhere between surprise and something I don't quite want to name. My skin still tingles where his lips touched, like the moment's trying to linger.

He holds the cookie up like it's a trophy he's won in some sportsball match and takes a bite.

"Ms. Wong, these are amazing." The coconut chocolate aroma of Darius's breath so close to my face intoxicates me. "I never realized you could bake like this."

"Yes, Darius, I have more skills than teaching music to children." She smiles wide, tilting her head so quickly, I'm certain her ponytail will whip around and smack her in the face, but it doesn't.

Darius jerks his head back, his mouth falling open,

exposing the half-chewed cookie and sensing the tension, I stand.

"Christine, maybe we should go to your room."

"No, no, I need to prep for third grade, anyway. If you hear a noise that sounds like a thousand swans slowly dying, it's just my class with recorders jammed into their mouths for the first time."

She gathers her things, including the remaining cookies, and heads for the door, turning before she leaves.

"*Damn Yankees*. Think about it."

And with that, she leaves me alone with Coach Hill.

"What's she so upset about?"

With Christine gone, he takes another bite of his cookie, crumbs falling right onto the name stitched on his tracksuit.

"Darius . . ." I gently reach out and brush away the tiny crumbs on his chest. "You have to understand, all that time you were picking on me, I wasn't the only one who noticed. You may have thought it was just playful teasing, but believe me, others noticed too."

"You mean Wong is mad at me, too?"

"Not mad. Just . . . cautious."

He nods and pulls his lips in. "Okay, I need to do more work with Christine. Got it."

"You don't have to do anything." I glance over and double-check that the door is closed before placing my hand on his thigh. "But it wouldn't hurt."

"But why is she so mad at the Yankees? Never would have pegged her for such a Red Sox fan."

"No, *Damn Yankees* is a musical. Christine couldn't care less about . . . basketball?"

With a massive grin, Darius swallows the last of his cookie. "Baseball, but gosh, you're cute."

He leans over, his chocolate coconut breath tickling my lips as he kisses me gently. Yeah, those soft, sweet lips might be the end of me.

"Door's not locked," I whisper as he pulls back.

"Harry, I don't care if the entire school knows how nuts I am for you."

I grab a pen from the caddy on the table and lean back in my chair. My fingers click the pen on and off as Darius stares at me with giant eyes. The finals are next weekend. I promised I'd chaperone. To help Coach Applegate and his puppies. The kids. For Darius. I have a ton of work to do before then, but that's over a week away, and I want to see him sooner.

"So, the finals," I begin, not sure how to ask. "You feeling ready for them?"

He shrugs, but his smile betrays a bit of nervous energy. "We will be. We have a few more practices between now and then. I don't want to overdo it, but I want to keep the boys' heads in the game."

"Sounds smart," I say.

"How about you? Ready for your next big chaperone gig?"

"I will be," I say, rubbing my temple. "I'm swamped. I've got essays to grade, meetings, prep work . . . It's gonna be a hell of a weekend."

Darius looks thoughtful for a moment before he says, "It sounds like you're going to be busy this weekend, but I've got tickets to the Mariners game next Wednesday. I'd love to take you. But I totally understand if your hands are full."

The idea of attending a professional sports game makes my skin crawl, but he's inviting me into his world. My lips press together as I stare at Darius's sweet face.

"I'd like that," I reply, fingers still clicking away on the pen.

Did I just agree to attend another sports event? My father would be shocked, then ecstatic. "But I want to see you before that."

"You do?"

I nod, biting my lower lip. "We could have another date." I'm already thinking about getting him alone. I inhale, leaning forward. "But this time at my place."

His eyes narrow slightly, like he's trying to figure me out. "Your place, huh? What's the occasion?"

I shrug, trying to act casual, though my pulse is quickening and blood rushes to my groin. "I thought maybe we could just hang out. How about Friday night? I'll order something."

He raises an eyebrow. "Friday night?"

"Yeah."

"Well, I've got practice Friday night. Maybe I can get Maynor to cover for me . . . depending on the puppies."

I try not to smile too wide, picturing him wrangling the boys. "What time does practice end?"

"Seven," he says, tapping his fingers on the arm of his chair.

"So . . . come after practice?" I ask, raising an eyebrow. My stomach twists with anticipation.

He looks like he's considering it for a second. "I'd need to go home and shower first."

"No, you don't," I say almost too quickly. "Just come over. You'll be fine."

The thought of Darius after practice, all sweaty and ripe, makes my dick lurch in my khakis.

His lips curl up at the corners, and he nods slowly. "Alright. I'll be there."

I grin, a little relief flooding through me. I've got him. "Perfect. I'll see you then."

"See you," he says, standing and giving me a knowing look before heading for the door.

My heart races as I watch him leave. His ass perfectly fills out those damn track pants. Excitement and nerves swirl in my torso. Friday night can't come soon enough.

11

HARRY

I GLANCE around my apartment as I stand in the bathroom, towel around my waist, steam curling up around me from the shower. The place is small, one bedroom, just the right size for me. It's neat—almost obsessively so. Every book on my shelves is lined up perfectly: classics on the left, modern novels on the right, a few poetry collections in the middle. Aside from the occasional stack of papers I need to grade, my desk in the corner of the room is always neat. I don't care for clutter. I prefer things in their place. It's comforting, even though I can get too caught up in the details.

I finish brushing my teeth, feeling the cool bristles against my gums, and quickly step out of the bathroom. A glance at the clock—6:45. Darius will be here soon, and I want to be ready. I slip on a pair of black jeans and a soft blue sweater, simple but crisp. Nothing flashy. I don't want to seem like I'm trying too hard, but I definitely want to look and feel good. Fresh. Clean.

I give my reflection one last check in the mirror and

then grab a mug and fill it with hot water and a tea bag. The warmth feels nice as I let it settle into my hands. I lean against the kitchen counter, waiting.

A soft knock on the door sends my heart skipping in my chest.

I'm already moving before I realize it, perhaps a little too eagerly. I open the door to find Darius standing there, a duffel bag slung over his shoulder. The bit of his hair escaping his baseball hat is matted, probably from practice. His cheeks are flushed, probably from the cold, and his eyes light up when he sees me.

"Hey," he says, voice low and warm, and before I can say anything, he's leaning in, brushing a soft kiss to my cheek.

"Hey, yourself," I answer, my pulse ramping up.

He looks past me, glancing around the apartment. "Nice and tidy, as expected."

I shrug, trying to act casual. "I prefer things to be organized."

He grins, takes off his coat, then holds out a large brown shopping bag he's been carrying. "Got you something."

I blink, a little thrown off. "You didn't have to do that."

"I wanted to," he says simply, his eyes twinkling. He steps inside, setting the bag on the kitchen counter. "Go ahead. Open it."

I pull the bag closer, curious. I'm not sure what to expect, but when I reach inside and pull out a pair of brand new ice skates, my breath catches.

"Darius . . ." I stare at them for a moment, a lump in my throat. "These are . . . amazing."

He watches me, his gaze soft but intense. "I figured you might want your own pair. They're not the hockey kind—these are for recreational skating. The ones you used last time seemed a little big." He pauses, then adds, "I checked your shoe size at the rink."

Those old skates he brought me fit just fine, but I'm not saying that. I let out a shaky breath, honestly a little overwhelmed by how thoughtful it is. "You really didn't have to, but . . . I love them." I swallow, feeling the sincerity of it all. "Thank you."

He smiles, the warmth in his eyes making my chest ache in the best way. "I'm glad you like them. We'll have to go skating again soon, so you can break them in."

I nod, and a wave of affection envelops me. "I'll be looking forward to it."

We fall into silence for a moment, but it's comfortable —easy. When he removes his warm-up jacket, his white T-shirt sticks to his body, and I do my best not to stare at his chest. He steps closer, his hand brushing against mine, and I find myself smiling again. "Dinner?" I ask, motioning to the pizza and salad I had delivered.

He grins and pats his stomach. "I've worked up an appetite from practice. And you know I never say no to food."

We eat at the small table in my kitchen, the pizza greasy and perfect, the salad barely touched except for the olives Darius picks out and pops into his mouth like a snack. I pilfer a few cherry tomatoes and do the same as he softly smiles at me from across the table. There's a quiet between us, but it's a comfortable kind—the kind that doesn't need filling. It's strange how easy it feels to be alone with him, but here we are. When we're done, we leave the plates where they are and move to the couch. I settle against the cushions, Darius pulling me close, his warmth seeping into me. Even though he appears to have cooled off from practice, he smells like sweat—musky, sharp, delicious.

He runs his fingers through my hair, and I close my eyes, just listening to the sound of his breathing. Then he kisses my forehead, lingering for a moment, and pulls back, giving me a teasing smile. "You know, you really look amazing tonight. Not that you don't usually. Just something's different. I like it."

I chuckle, a little embarrassed. "It's because I'm not dressed for school. I'm not always so buttoned-up."

He shakes his head, his expression sincere. "Maybe that's it. But, I'm serious. You look . . . perfect."

I feel my pulse quicken at the way he's looking at me, like I'm dessert. I can't help it. I slide my hand up his thigh, leaning closer. "You smell . . ." I murmur, not able to hide the grin pulling at my lips.

"I know. I told you I needed to shower."

"I was going to say, amazing. You smell amazing." I run my nose up his neck to the back of his head, taking him in.

He laughs softly, clearly enjoying the way we're teasing each other, but then his tone shifts, soft and serious. "Harry, you're getting me all worked up."

I smile, feeling like my whole body's been lit up, and then, in the quiet of my apartment, Darius leans in again, pressing his lips gently to mine. And I'm gone, completely. Everything else fades into the background—the apartment, the books, the open pizza box and dishes on the table—but him? Him, I want to keep close. I want this. I want us.

"Good." I squeeze his thigh right above his knee. "If you're all worked up, maybe I can work you over."

He coughs, and fuck, I love messing with him.

"Did you want me to . . . clean up? I showered before practice, but I could definitely use another. Do you have a towel I can use?"

"Nope. I want you just like this." I lift his arm, burying my face in his sweaty pit. His white T-shirt is damp under his arm, clinging to his skin. "Right here. You okay with that, Coach?"

He nods quickly, then swallows hard. "Yup. More than okay."

I straddle him, lift both arms above his head, clasping him by the wrists.

"Perfect."

12

HARRY

I'VE GOT Darius exactly where I want him. His wrists are together, held tightly by my left hand. I'm not trying to hurt him, but a small part of me enjoys having him under my control this way. A tinge of skin peeks through his lifted shirt, and he smells like a locker room. Yum.

"Let's get this dirty shirt off you," I say, tugging at the hem with my free hand. He moves to pull his hat off, but I stop him. "Leave it on."

The shirt ends up over his head. I release his wrists, and he tugs it off, tossing it by the edge of the couch. His hat comes off too, but he grabs it and puts it back on—backwards.

"You're such a fucking dudebro," I say.

"Thank you." He scrunches his eyebrows in this ridiculously charming way. "I think."

Something inside me smolders seeing his naked chest again. That soft brown hair, dusted across his pecs, leading right down to the treasure in his track pants.

"I wanna lick you up and down," I say.

"Go for it, Harry. Lick away."

A snort escapes my lips. He's trying to be sexy, but he just comes off as silly—which is, ironically, more sexy.

I smash my mouth onto his, our tongues meeting in the middle. There's no pretense as I straddle him. My hands take in the light fur on his chest before finding his nipples—pinching, getting them nice and hard for my mouth.

Before moving to his chin, I give his bottom lip a bite and a little tug until he winces.

"Now, be a good coach for me. Can you do that?"

"Yes, sir."

My tongue runs down his neck, right between his pecs, before selecting the right one to start with. I take his nipple in my mouth, circling it, flicking, and taking tiny nibbles. After a few seconds, I switch to sucking then go back to using my tongue and teeth. By the noises coming out of his mouth, I'm fairly certain it's driving Darius wild.

"Fuck, Harry. You're making me so damn hard."

Bingo.

I reach down between his legs, and sure enough, the firm bulge in his track pants confirms his statement.

"Good," I say, pulling off his chest. "Hard is the goal."

I glance up and give him a smirk, and he runs his index finger over my lips.

"Goal? Are you talking sports to turn me on?"

His cock throbs in my hand, and he returns my smile. I take his finger in my mouth, ready to bite it, but Darius swirls it inside, and instead I take a few long sucks, giving him a preview of what's coming.

"Harry, you're going to be the end of me."

My eyebrows wiggle up, and I give his finger another swirl of my tongue before pulling off and returning to his torso. I'm on his stomach now, letting his treasure trail lead me right to the pot of gold waiting at the end of the Coach Hill rainbow. Wanting to tease him a bit, I don't take his pants off yet. Instead, I run my mouth over his cock, the synthetic fabric—polyester would be my guess—smooth and sleek as I gnaw at the head of his dick.

"Harry, please. My cock, I'm . . ."

He's shaking under me, my lips adding pressure as I glide down the shaft, then back up and nibble right under the head, in that super sensitive spot.

"Okay, okay," I say. "Lift." I pat his ass.

Darius does as I ask, and I yank his pants down and off his ankles. Instead of his cock popping up, though, it's still under fabric. The head, barely poking out from the waistband of his jockstrap, leaks precum. I toss his pants on top of the jacket next to the couch and lean over, sucking right at the tip.

"Sorry. I don't really need to wear one to coach, but I'm just used to putting them on for anything athletic. It's a habit from college." He moves his hands to the waistband. "Let me take it off."

I put my hands on his, stopping him. "Not yet."

His eyes widen and a small laugh escapes his lips. "Oh? Does Mr. Peterson have a jockstrap fantasy?"

"Maybe."

I'm not sure where the association comes from—jockstraps are sports-related, sure. But I remember a few guys wearing them in the locker room back in high school, and the memory rushes back as I run my tongue along the top of the support pouch. When I get to his balls, he shifts, and says, "Harry, are you sure you don't want me to take a shower? I can be real quick. I promise."

"Coach." I glide my thumb under the waistband, adding pressure to the head, and he squirms with delight. "I want you sweaty."

"Oh. Okay, then."

I stand and realize, while Darius may be almost naked, I'm still completely dressed. Quickly, I'm out of my jeans, my briefs clinging onto my frame as my cock tries to escape the waistband, just like his. When I pull my sweater and shirt over my head, fingers grab onto the elastic of my underwear and tug. He's still on the couch, dragging me between his legs, eyes focused on my midsection.

"Harry, I want to suck your cock so bad." His fingers crawl inside, grazing the tip. "Can I? Please?"

"I mean, since you asked so politely."

I pull my briefs off, adding them to the growing pile on the floor. And then Darius, with permission granted, leans forward and takes me in his mouth—almost to the base. He didn't get a chance to blow me at the hotel, and I'm impressed by his skills. There's some gulping and gagging noises, but he's not backing off—between the noises and enthusiasm he's bringing, I'm sensing he's simply enjoying himself.

My fingers grip the sides of his head. There's not a ton of hair to get lost in, but the peach fuzz on his buzzed sides is soft, and I latch on to his ears, plunging myself down his throat, and watching his lips stretch around me as he goes to town.

"You like sucking my dick, Coach?"

He moans his answer, and I throw my head back, taking in the absolute pleasure of fucking the face of the man who tormented me for years. Yeah, turns out he had a massive crush on me, and it was all to get my attention, but nevertheless, he's now choking on my cock.

He pulls off, wiping saliva from his mouth. "Okay, Peterson. I need a breather."

I swivel around and drag the small coffee table to the edge of the area rug. There's more room now as a plan formulates in my head. I grab a throw pillow from the sofa for my head and lie down in the newly open space.

"Stand over me, please," I say from the floor.

Darius complies, straddling my body, facing me, I can see his poor dick still desperate to escape the jockstrap.

"Now turn around." I grab my cock, giving it a few tugs as he does as I ask.

"Look at that thick, juicy ass in those straps. So damn delicious, Darius."

"Really?"

"Abso-fucking-lutely."

He shakes his ass a little, the thick muscle framed by the bands of fabric jiggles, and my dick throbs in my grip.

"Fuck, you're hot."

He laughs at this, and I'm pretty sure nobody's ever told him how sexy he is. I mean, the whole athletic suit, baseball hat, PE teacher machismo stuff aside. Nah, it's all that, too.

"Now listen Darius, I want you to sit back. Carefully."

He turns around, eyebrows jogging up his forehead, trying to hide behind the back of his hat.

"Sit on you?"

"Well, my face to be exact. Come." I pat my chest. "Get on your knees."

He squats down, straddling my torso, knees on the rug, and without even touching him, his ass spreads, exposing the beautiful hole I finger banged in Rhode Island. It was dark in the hotel room, and I didn't get the best view. Now, I'm witnessing a damn work of art.

"Look at your pretty hole."

"Pretty?" He glances over his shoulder but can't quite make eye contact.

"Yes, Darius, your asshole is pretty. Beautiful. Gorgeous. Spectacular. Exquisite." I slap his right cheek. "I'm an English teacher with a thesaurus fetish. I can keep going."

This makes him laugh, his ass jiggling with each chuckle.

"Now, get back here."

With my hands on his waist, I guide him back until I'm able to make contact with my tongue. Darius lets out a small gasp, and I wait, inhaling deeply, taking in the musky scent of him. He may have showered earlier, but whatever running around he did at practice has him all sweaty. Go Sharks!

"Ease back," I tell him. "I've got you."

And then, doing as he's told, Darius lets his weight rest on my face. With the help of gravity, I'm able to glide my tongue inside him, swirling around, tasting the sweet perspiration as his hole opens up for me. With my hands occupied, holding him in place and spreading him open, I'm unable to reach my aching cock. I can feel the precum on my stomach, and I thrust my hips up slightly, hoping Darius takes the hint.

I pull back for a breath, panting with pleasure.

"Grind into my face."

Fingers wrap around my dick, stroking slowly, as I continue devouring him, and when I hear him spit, adding some slickness to his hand, I reward him by burying my tongue even deeper. Then, with his free hand, Darius reaches back, losing his hand in my curls, tugging, pulling me up, inside his perfect hole. We find a steady rhythm, him jerking me while pushing back, fucking my mouth with his ass.

"Peterson, fuck." He moves forward, and I pull back, replacing my tongue with two fingers. "You're blowing my mind."

"Remember when you wanted to fuck me in Rhode Island?"

My fingers are inside him, just past the knuckles, clearly doing a good job, because with the next plunge, his entire body trembles. He fucking trembles.

Darius pauses the attention he's giving my cock. "Yeah."

"Get me ready, Coach. I want to tap in."

I bend my knees, then lift my legs, giving him access to my ass, and like a good coach, he leans forward, spitting on his fingers and teasing my hole.

"Hang on," I say.

Hoping this would happen, I planted supplies under the sofa. With a quick swipe, I grab the tube of lube and pass it to him. "Here. Get me ready for your fat cock."

"It's fat?"

"Thick. Meaty. Plentiful. Perfect. Shall I continue?"

He laughs, and the cap clicks open. I hear him squirt lube onto his hand, and then he's inside me. A single finger at first. He's being gentle, careful. I take the lube from the rug and apply some to my fingers and his hole. He's open from the rimming, and with the addition of lube, I easily slide three fingers in.

"Like this," I say. "Open me up."

He adds another finger, going deeper, mimicking what I'm doing to him.

"This good?"

"Fuck, Darius, yes. It feels amazing. Go for it."

With that, he goes further. Spreading my ass, adding a third finger as my pelvis raises higher, urging him on.

"Darius, I want you to fuck me. Hard. Fuck me like you've wanted to for the last four years. You up for that, Coach?"

He twists his fingers inside me, my hole hungry for more. "Hell, yes."

Darius

13

DARIUS

THIS IS NOT what I expected after the last week with Harry. He was just starting to let me in, the dinner and skating was so . . . innocent. Sweet. Holding hands on the ice. Kissing in my car in front of his building. When he invited me over, I figured we'd eat some pizza and watch a smarty-pants movie that would fly over my head.

Nope. Instead, I'm in my jockstrap, squatting over his face, while we both finger bang each other into oblivion.

It's fucking hot as hell. Harry, with those damn curls and innocent face bossing me around. Smelling every inch of me, even though I'm a sweaty mess from practice. People think coaching peewee means you're just on the sides screaming at the kids the entire time. It's actually the opposite. I demonstrate every movement, making sure they understand the technique and feel confident before trying it themselves. It's my job to actively engage and guide them through each step, creating a learning environment where they can absorb and mimic the skills in real time.

Kinda like what Harry's doing right now with my hole.

"Fuck, Harry, you're, you're . . ."

"You like that, Coach?"

He's got at least two fingers inside me. But he's not just pounding away like some straight dude in a porno. Harry's got a technique, and he's, well, coaching me.

His fingers are rotating as he moves them in and out. And he's not pulling them all the way out. He leaves them in, simply gliding them back and forth. The lube helps him go deeper, but every so often, he spits too. Saliva on its own isn't going to do the trick, but a saliva chaser on top of lube works surprisingly well. He's using his free hand to keep me spread, allowing the one inside me to go further, and while I've never experienced it before, I'm fairly certain he's hitting my prostate, because my hips are shaking in a way that's never happened before, and there's precum leaking out of my cock like a dripping faucet.

"Harry, if you want me to fuck you, you need to stop."

Without a word, he pulls out, slapping my ass cheek before leaning forward and kissing it. He lowers his legs, and my fingers slip out of him. All three of them. He's more than ready to take me.

He pats my ass again, giving me a little nudge, and I move off him.

"I need a quick drink of water. Want some?"

I'm not really thirsty, but I also know it's a good idea to hydrate during strenuous activities.

"Okay."

I move to the couch and watch Harry push himself up. He heads to a cabinet in the kitchen, his boner bouncing as he walks.

He's behind me now, but I can hear water from the sink, followed by him washing his hands and filling the glasses.

"You okay if I take this jock off?" I pull on the waistband, my dick eager for freedom.

He's behind me, presenting a small glass of water over my shoulder. I take it, and he leans down, kissing my neck, making all sorts of new nerves come alive. "Wait. Let me do it."

Harry sits next to me. Not on the other side of the couch, but right next to me. The entire side of his body is plastered against mine, like we're connected by sticky tape. He's out of breath—probably from being suffocated by my ass, and he gulps his water quickly.

"Before we . . . move on, let's chat about sexual health." He takes the last sip of his water, and sets his glass down on the coffee table he moved to the edge of the rug. "I haven't had a boyfriend . . . in a long time."

"Harry, you're twenty-eight."

"Since high school. But I've dated. Had some encounters. I'm tested regularly. Clear results across the board."

A burning ignites in my core, thinking of Harry with other men. I take a sip of my water attempting to extinguish it and smile. I have no right being jealous.

"I haven't been with anyone in three years," I say. "I get tested at my yearly physical, which was last summer."

Harry edges forward, reaches under the couch, and

pulls out a strip of condoms. "Let's use these. Just to be safe. If things . . . continue, we can talk more about it. Sound good?"

He holds the condoms up, and they fall. There's four of them. I'm not sure what he's expecting, but I nod. "Sure. Of course. Happy to suit up."

"How about I put it on for you?"

"Um, sure. Okay."

Harry takes my almost empty glass and puts it on the table next to his. When he returns to the sofa, he pushes my legs apart and kneels before me. My dick, still raging hard and desperate to escape the confines of the jockstrap, becomes even firmer as his fingers crawl under the waistband and brush against the tip.

With a quick glance and a smirk so delicious I could eat it for dinner, Harry pulls the fabric down, finally freeing my cock.

"There we go." He runs his fingers over it, catching the precum on this thumb and rubbing it against the head. "You're horny."

"Yeah, how'd you figure that out?"

He pulls my entire shaft back, then lets it go. A loud slap echoes in the room. "Lucky guess."

With a quick rip, Harry removes the condom, holds my erection up, and places it at the tip. It slides down easily, a snug fit, but there will be no complaints from me. He squirts some lube on me then nods, and I take over, spreading the lube over my cock, while he adds more to his ass.

"How did you want to . . ." My dick pulses in my hand, so ready to be inside him.

"Let's start like this." He pushes me against the back cushions of the sofa. "I'll ride you."

He raises his eyebrows, and I nod. Perhaps a little too eagerly.

Harry climbs on my lap, his knees near my waist straddling me, reaches back, and grasps my cock. He places it at his hole then rests his palms on my chest.

"Easy now," he says.

I take hold of his waist. Peering up at him like this, with the light from the kitchen shrouding him, he looks like a fucking angel. I'm not religious, but right now, I feel like I should pray and thank someone.

"I'm in no rush, Harry."

My thumb coasts over his hip bone, trying to take in every ounce of him. After all these years, it's happening. Well, it sort of happened at the semi-finals, but this is something different. Not because of the fucking. Because we're in his place. We've been on a real date. Dinner. Skating. He asked me over. We had pizza and salad. This is more.

As he guides me in, he bites at his lower lip. He's slow at first, taking some deep breaths, waiting, then accepting more. I had three of my fingers inside him, no problem, but my cock is fatter. Longer. Harder. I do my best to focus on Harry's beautiful face. His body connecting with mine. But really, being inside him this way, my dick feels like it's marching in a damn ticker-tape parade.

"There we go," he says. He's lowered himself down. I'm completely inside him. "You okay?"

"Me?" I ask, trying to ignore the fluttering in my belly. "Better than okay. I'm fantastic. Harry, this is . . ."

"Awesome." He pushes a long breath out of pursed lips.

"Yeah, awesome. Does it feel good?" My eyes scan his face, his mouth so fucking beautiful I want to take a picture and make it my phone's background.

He nods, eyes focused on mine. "Darius, you feel amazing."

There's a smile on his face when he says it, and I can feel him relaxing, letting my cock settle inside him.

"Harry. You . . . you . . ." My mind zooms, searching for the right words to convey how he feels. Not just the sex, but him. Being in his place. So close. Connected to him in a way I only dreamed about. "You really have to know how sorry I am. About being a jerk. About teasing you. I was crushing on you so bad, and, and . . ."

"Coach." He places a finger over my lips. "No more apologizing. You've already made it up to me."

I kiss the tip of his finger then take it in my mouth, gently sucking as he picks up the pace, his hard-on bobbing like a buoy while he bounces on my dick. I'm focused on the feeling, the pleasure, being inside him, and then Harry starts making these noises. It sounds like a whimper but then kind of morphs into a moan. He's thrown his head back, clearly enjoying himself—which only makes me harder.

"Peterson. I've wanted you since you walked into the teacher's lounge talking about wanting to fuck Wolverine."

I lift my hips, plunging into him as he massages my chest, eyes rolling back.

"Wolverine?" This seems to bring him out of his sex stupor. "Huh?"

"Nothing. I was just saying I've wanted you for a long time. Since that first day you were talking about Wolverine."

"Are you trying to turn me on more by talking about Hugh Jackman?"

Without letting go of Harry's hips, my thrusting pauses. "Are you really talking about how hot you think Wolverine is while I'm literally inside you?"

He shrugs, leans over and plants a sloppy kiss on my mouth.

When he pulls back I say, "I'm not jealous of Wolverine. He may have giant claws, but I've got this."

I move my hands down, spreading his ass wide, and ram my dick deep. The moan that comes out of Harry's mouth sends shivers down my spine, and he bends to reward me with another kiss.

"How about a new position, Coach?"

"What did you have in mind?"

Harry carefully dismounts me, gives my cock a quick stroke, grabs my half full glass from the coffee table, and gulps it down.

"Between your fingers and riding you, you've opened me right up." He wipes his mouth, returns the glass, then bends over the couch.

He crosses his arms over the cushions on the back, pulls his knees on the sofa, and juts his ass out. With a glance over his shoulder, he says, "C'mere, Coach. Ready to hammer me home?"

"Fuck, Harry."

I stand and move behind him, taking in the view before resuming.

"What's wrong? Do we need more lube?" He grabs the tube from the sofa and hands it back.

"No. I mean, maybe. Sure." I take it, squirting some on my dick and rubbing it around the shaft. "I just wanna look at you for a second."

He arches his back, exposing his hole. My hands are on him, massaging, spreading, rubbing the tip of my cock on his opening, but not entering him yet. I want to take a moment to appreciate his beautiful butt.

"Your ass is absolutely perfect, Harry. This ass exceeds all the standards. Extra credit for the tiny bit of fuzz around the perimeter." I run my thumb around it, teasing him. "As long as I've lusted after you, I never imagined it would be this magnificent."

He wiggles his ass a little, and I slap my dick on his right cheek, then place it in position but don't go further.

"You want it, Harry? You want me to fuck your gorgeous hole?"

"Please, Coach. Get in there. Now."

As he pushes back, my cock slides in effortlessly, the familiar warmth and pressure comforting my entire soul.

"Hold on," he says. "Don't move. Let me take over for a minute."

Unsure what he wants me to do, I let go of him and place my hands behind my head. Harry turns around and eyes me up and down.

"Fuck, Darius. Stay just like that. With your pits showing." He takes a deep inhale. "Just like that."

And then he moves back, taking me all the way in. I

do as I'm told, keeping my hands where they are, and Harry fucks my dick as I get completely lost in the complete bliss coursing through my veins.

"Use my cock, Harry. Fuck it with that sweet ass."

This spurs him on. He's moving faster, and the sensation is like nothing I've felt before. He's doing all the work, and I don't know what I can do. So I talk.

"You're doing such a good job, Harry. Fucking me like this. That's it. Good job. So good."

I leave one hand behind my head, and reach over with the other, running my fingers through his curls.

"Grab it," he says. "My hair. Pull it—lightly."

My fingers grasp on, and I do as he asks. Harry's head falls back, and he continues fucking me while I tug gently on his hair.

"This okay?" I ask.

"Fuck, yes." He pauses, his body heavy with breath. "Okay, you can take over now. I'm tapping you in, Coach."

I laugh at him trying to sound like he knows anything about sports and grab onto his waist with one hand. I pull him back, and he spreads his knees a little wider.

"There we go," I say. "Get ready for a pounding."

I reach around with my free hand, and his cock is so hard. So wet. I give him a few strokes, the precum making it slick, and Harry moans, arching his back and bucking into me as I jerk him. My heart hammers in my chest, knowing he's loving this as much as me.

I lean over, moving my mouth closer to his neck, and pepper it with kisses. "Damn, Harry. You're so fucking sexy. So fucking hot. I wanna rail you like this forever."

I'm pretty sure the noises he's making—a low rumble of consent—mean he agrees with everything I'm saying. The air vibrates with his desperate whimpers and moans, building the heat until it happens. That tiny scratch deep inside my core signals my orgasm is on its way.

"Good, don't stop," he says. "Harder, Darius. I love your dick inside me. Plowing me."

"Harry, I'm close. Do you want me to . . ."

I've got the condom on. I could keep going, come inside him. I'm unsure what he wants me to do. All I know is I want whatever Harry wants.

"Wait."

He turns around so quickly, I almost miss it. My cock points straight at him as he situates himself on the sofa, facing me. He seizes me, holding the base near my balls, and tugs the condom off.

"I want it. Here."

He points to his face.

"Um, okay. It won't take but a second." I stroke myself and notice Harry's doing the same.

"Tell me when you're close."

I stand there, my orgasm crawling up, a wave of incredible, almost overwhelming pleasure building. Harry jerks himself, but his eyes are focused on me. Well, my dick.

My pelvis begins to tighten, followed by the rest of my body as my heartbeat reaches a fever pitch. I'm staring at Harry. His beautiful face. Eyes. Lips. That soft, blond curly hair. And that's it. I'm on the edge of a cliff, about to freefall.

I nod but then realize, he's not looking at my face. "I'm close. Now. It's . . ."

Harry lets go of himself and grabs on, first over my hand, but I quickly let go and he takes over, using both hands to pump. It only takes two strokes, and I come undone. My eyes close, head falls back, and I'm drowned in a sudden, intense tsunami of pleasure.

Maybe because it's been so long since I've fucked someone. Or maybe because it's Harry. Or maybe a little of both. But there's a lot. Buckets. It just keeps flowing, and by the fourth or fifth spurt, I'm chuckling, overtaken by the complete bliss of it all.

But even after I've finished, he doesn't relent.

"Harry, I'm good."

There's more laughing, but Harry doesn't stop. When I look down, he's plastered. His chest. Shoulder. Face. Hair.

"Oh, gosh. Harry. I'm so sorry."

I lift his chin, taking in the damage. His right eye is closed and covered. He's kind of stuck this way, and I look around, searching for something to clean him up with.

"Sorry for what? I was the one draining every last drop out of you."

"Fair. Let me get you something . . . do you want to use my shirt?"

"No, I'm good." He wipes his eye, blinks it a few times, and there he is.

Covered in cum, but just as fucking beautiful.

"What about you?"

"I came. Right before you. You didn't even notice."

He nods down, and when I glance at my shins, yup, covered in it.

"We're a mess," I say.

"That's easily rectified. How about that shower you wanted before?"

He stands, and, with his entire face slathered in my seed, gives me the softest kiss—as if this, somehow, is still tender. Still sacred. He takes my hand without hesitation and leads me down the hall to the bathroom.

The air between us hums with something unspoken, something fragile and real. And as the door closes behind us, I realize—mess or not, this feels like the beginning of something worth cleaning up for.

14

DARIUS

THE SHEETS TANGLE around us as we lie in Harry's bed, skin still warm from the shower, bodies close but not quite touching. Being this close, it's like the electricity from what just happened still sparks between us, and I'm so fucking tempted to grab him and pull him on top of me to snuggle . . . or maybe more. The soft rustle of Harry's breath greets me as he turns to face me, one arm tucked behind his head. His curls are wet, more defined, and the sandy blond hair in his armpit contrasts with his pale skin. God, he's so damn beautiful, it hurts.

The dim light from the bedside table casts a shadow across his face, but I can still make out the gentle curve of his lips, forming the hint of a smile.

"That was . . ." He trails off, eyes lingering on mine. His voice is low, yet it carries the weight of something deeper than mere satisfaction with the phenomenal banging we just shared.

"Amazing," I finish for him, grinning.

My heart still hasn't settled from the rush of the

evening. The impact of what happened tonight still coursing through me with a charged energy. The sex. The shower. Harry lying on his bed next to me while water drips from his forehead. I thought I knew what intimacy was, but this? This feels entirely new.

He laughs softly, his chest rumbling, drawing my attention. Besides the few hairs surrounding his nipples, he's as smooth as a freshly waxed sports car. My tongue skates across my lips, watching him. He's so fucking lickable.

"Yeah. Definitely amazing," he says.

I roll onto my stomach to get more comfortable, but mostly to be closer to him. He brushes a hand over my head, his fingers landing on my ear, rubbing and squeezing. The way Harry took control—it was nothing like my brief relationship in college. Doug was . . . well, he was insecure, hesitant. We never really seemed on the same wavelength. Sure, I was hanging out with my hockey teammates, and Doug was usually with the theatre crowd, but it was more than that. We never seemed to truly connect. Even when we were alone.

But Harry? There's something about the way he looks at me. The way he moves. He just knows what I want without me having to ask for it. He doesn't question. He just does. And fuck, it feels so damn good.

"You know, this"—I move my hands between us—"is way different than with my ex." The words slip out before I can even think about it, and I swallow hard, wishing I could gobble them back up.

Harry cocks an eyebrow and moves the hand behind his head so he's opening himself, an invitation. I lay my head on his chest, and fuck, lying on him this way feels like heaven.

"Different, how?"

I don't want Harry to think I'm rushing things. Or comparing him to someone else. And honestly, there's no comparison. The hotel room. What we just did. It's monumentally different.

"It just feels more . . . real, I guess. Is that weird?"

"No."

His fingers play with the hair at the top of my head. It's not much, but it's longer than the buzzed sides and back, and for the first time in ages, I find myself contemplating whether I should let it grow longer.

"With Doug, I always felt like I was tiptoeing around him. In bed, we were like two baby lambs fumbling to find our footing. Kinda like you on the ice."

He punches my arm softly. "Hey, I wasn't that bad."

"Harry." I grab his hand from my head, kissing across his knuckles. "You were perfect."

He smiles, and his radiant expression makes my heart sing.

"With you . . ." I continue. "You just *know*. You know exactly what you want and tell me what to do, and honestly, I never realized how much I would love that."

Harry exhales, a hint of a laugh in his chest. "Well, I'm glad it's working for you."

He resumes massaging my scalp.

"It is," I blurt. "But it's not only that. It's the way you . . . take control. It makes me feel safe, like I can just let go and enjoy myself because I'm in excellent hands. I've never felt that way before."

His fingers pause, and I think he might say something, but he's quiet. This shift in his mood doesn't go unnoticed, and my chest twists. Something's off.

"Hey," I nudge his side, trying to catch his attention again. "I want to know something. After the semi-finals . . . back at school, you were distant. Like, you pushed me away. I was excited to keep things going, but . . . I don't know . . . Did I do something wrong?"

He shifts slightly, and I glance up to see him staring at the ceiling. Anticipation curls around me.

"I was scared," he whispers. "I had fun in Rhode Island. Clearly. But I guess the idea of getting too close scares me. I've . . . I've been burned by someone like you before."

"Burned?" I echo, trying to piece together what he means.

"My high school boyfriend. Peter." Harry pauses. He takes a deep inhale, his breath hitching. "We weren't exactly out. Not fully, anyway. My family knew, and I was trying to be more out at school. Peter wasn't having it. We fought about it. All I wanted was to make him happy. Then . . . something happened." He stares at the ceiling, blinking. "Someone on his track team found out and confronted Peter. He denied it. The whole thing blew up in my face. He wouldn't talk to me. I mean, he wouldn't even look at me." Harry's eyes meet mine, and my body vibrates with sadness for high school Harry. "The game. It brought up all these insecurities I have. I think I was scared of . . . of what could happen if it all went wrong again."

His words sink into me, and a strange pain burns in

my chest. My heart aches for him, for the past that still haunts him. For younger Harry. I sit up, face him, and hold his arm. My fingers brush his soft skin, and my thumb rubs tiny circles on the underside of his forearm.

"I didn't want that to happen with you," Harry continues, his eyes finally meeting mine again. "I didn't want to mess this up."

I reach out, grasping his shoulders. "You didn't mess anything up, Harry. Not with me."

He takes in a deep breath and then lets it out slowly. "You mean it?"

"Yeah," I say firmly, my voice steady. "I mean it. I'm out at work. Just because your gaydar is on the fritz doesn't mean others don't know."

"Really?"

"I'm not wearing a rainbow tracksuit, but I'm not ashamed."

"You should. Wear a rainbow tracksuit, I mean. You'd look great."

I laugh at the thought and lean my head into his hand.

"Okay, now, can you please elaborate on why you were a massive prick to me for the last four years?"

My eyes dart down as my ears burn hot. "I told you, I had a crush on you."

"Darius." Harry places a finger under my chin, lifts it, and forces my gaze to meet his. "For four years you teased me because you liked me? You're not ten."

"I . . . didn't know how to show it. At school. I know what most people think of me. Coach Hill. The PE teacher. Hockey coach. Always wearing the same damn tracksuit. Most of them probably assume I'm straight." I put my hand up quickly. "Not because I've ever said that. Or even hinted at it. But people just make their own stories up about you based on what they think they know. Anyway, I guess I was trying to hide it. Not being gay. My feelings. For you." My head spins as my mouth tries to keep up. "Harry, you're so damn smart. Confident. Loudly out. Handsome. You're everything I wish I could be. I thought someone like you would never go for a guy like me so, I was a . . . what did you say, again?"

"A prick."

"Right. I was a prick."

"But Darius, that's where you're wrong. I mean, I am smart. Handsome enough." He smiles and my stomach flips. "You're wrong about someone like me never going for a guy like you."

My eyes flutter. Trying to see him more clearly in the low light. Blinking away the wetness and hoping Harry doesn't see. And then he takes my face in his hands. Holding my jaw like a soccer ball, and something amazing happens. Harry looks at me in this way, like he really sees me—all of me. And that look makes everything else not matter.

A gentle smile plucks at the corner of his lips, and a cozy warmth spreads through me. It's like everything—every worry, every fear—melts away in the space between us.

He shifts slightly, pulling me closer, his hand resting gently on the back of my neck. "Stay over?" he asks, his voice soft but hopeful. "It's Friday. We don't have to do anything else. Just . . . be here. With me."

I nod before I can even think about it. The thought of being with him tonight, of staying at his place, holding him all night, feels like the most natural thing in the world. "Yeah, I'd like that."

We settle back into the warmth of the bed, the silence wrapping around us like a blanket. His arm slips around me, pulling me close. As I close my eyes, the steady beat of his heart against mine lulls me into a perfect peace I never realized I was missing.

For the first time in a long time, I'm exactly where I'm supposed to be.

Harry

15

HARRY

I'M STANDING before the whiteboard, trying to ignore the mild panic creeping up through my shoulders. This isn't the typical Monday morning blues. It's something else. Something to do with a certain PE teacher and coach who always wears a tracksuit and baseball cap and possesses a perfectly sized cock.

I should be focusing on the lesson plan for the day. *Lord of the Flies*. Civilization vs. savagery. The characters had every intention to act civilized, but what makes them devolve into savagery? The kids will have a lot to say about it. Savage. Untamed. Raw. Like the way Darius pounded me on my sofa. Fuck.

I need to focus on the day ahead, but my silly brain keeps bouncing back to Friday night. Saturday morning. Coach Darius Hill.

Darius, who held me so tightly that I was convinced he'd never let me go—like his entire existence depended on it. Between the sex and cuddling, he managed to make me feel both unraveled and safe at the same time. How is that even possible? Is that how other people feel? Please let it be how other people feel, because wow.

And then Saturday morning—the pancakes. Soft, fluffy clouds of breakfast deliciousness. I wasn't sure I had the ingredients, but Darius managed to scrounge up what he needed. I'm not sure if flour expires, but neither of us has gotten sick so far. He had flour all over his face by the time he was done, and honestly, it was the cutest. I tried to make a joke about it, but he just grinned like he didn't care about anything other than making me breakfast.

It's like I'm soaring above the clouds. Not in a plane. Just me. Gliding as the air whooshes around me and the world spins beneath me.

With a shake of my head, I pull myself together and focus on the pen in my hand. I write "*Lord of the Flies*, Themes" in big, bold letters, but my mind ricochets back to how Darius looked in my kitchen. Tossing him into the tub and pouring maple syrup all over him seemed like a viable option. I'm usually not one to miss clues, so how did I overlook the signs that he fancied me all these years?

"Knock, knock."

The voice breaks me out of my reverie. I turn to see Christine stepping into the classroom with her usual half-closed smile. She may be my best friend around here, but . . . well, that's exactly the reason she's not running for president of Darius' fan club anytime soon.

"Good morning, friend. How was your weekend?" I ask, trying really hard to hide the sex afterglow I'm afraid is written all over my face.

She rolls her eyes dramatically. "Well, Denise threw

up on the one tiny rug in my bathroom. Not on the tile, not on the wood floor—nope, the rug. It's like she knows that's the one place not to do it and seeks it out. So I woke up having to do laundry before school, which, you know, is fantastic." She gives a little shrug, as if it's not the least bit tragic.

I grin. "Well, at least it wasn't on your bed. Could've been worse."

"You have no idea. That rug is like . . . one square foot. Why can't she be a normal cat?" She shakes her head in mock disbelief. "Honestly, I'm thinking of giving her away. Not like she'd care."

I chuckle. "I'm sure she'd care. Denise adores you. And she'd just puke somewhere else in protest."

"Probably," she agrees, still shaking her head. "Anyway, that's my morning. How about you? How's the whole Darius situation progressing?"

My stomach flutters at the mention of his name, but I do my best to keep it cool. "It's . . . good," I say, making a little circular motion with my hand, like I'm trying to catch the right words in the air. "Honestly? Better than good. We're figuring it out. I'm trying to get over my deep-seated fear of anything sports-related, and he's been, well, trying. More open, more—" I stop myself. I don't want to sound like I'm gushing, but it's hard not to after the weekend. "Just . . . more."

Christine narrows her eyes, folding her arms over her chest. "More what? I don't know, Harry. After everything he's done. Wouldn't you prefer someone who treats you like a prince from the beginning rather than someone who suddenly changes once he recognizes his mistakes?"

I sigh, reminding myself Christine cares about me. She doesn't want me to get hurt.

"I get that, I really do," I say, leaning against the desk in the front row. "But I think he was just . . . insecure. He actually told me he never thought someone like me would go for someone like him." I purse my lips and wait for her cool expression to shift. It doesn't. "I'm not making excuses for the way he treated me—believe me, I've had my share of conversations with him about that—but he's trying, Christine. He made me pancakes."

She doesn't seem convinced, her arms still crossed as she studies me. "And you think fluffy carbs are enough? After all the years he treated you like trash?"

I bite my lip, thinking it over. "I think it's enough for now. It's like the kids. The way Victor picks on Rebecca. You've seen that, right?"

"Yes, but Darius isn't a ten-year-old boy."

"Fair. But he apologized. Many times. He bought me ice skates." I give her my best pleading smile. "Can you please give him a chance? I'm not saying you have to be best friends, but just . . . try."

Christine sighs, clearly not thrilled with this request, but she uncrosses her arms and stands. "I'll try. But you're my chief concern, Harry. If he hurts you, I can't be held responsible for my actions."

"Plot twist. The music teacher is a badass."

"Damn right." She makes some martial arts move I don't know with her hands, and we both smile.

"Who's a badass?"

My stomach flips at the sound of his voice, and then I see his hazel eyes and that damn tracksuit.

"Me," Christine says. "Did you have any doubt?"

Darius walks in and stops near the table, forming a triangle between the three of us.

"Listen, anyone who can make a third-grade recorder concert bearable—let alone enjoyable—is the very definition of a badass."

Christine glares at him, and I take a deep breath, waiting for her reply.

"True." She pulls her lips in, and I can almost see the wheels in her head turning. "The recorder is the most misunderstood instrument."

"Exactly," Darius says.

A half smile meanders onto Christine's face, and she turns toward me and winks.

"Well, gentlemen, I have to go get the boomwhackers ready."

"Another critically undervalued instrument," Darius says.

At the door, Christine pauses and turns to face us. "Don't push your luck."

"Noted," Darius says with a nod.

Christine leaves, carefully closing the door behind her, and we're alone.

"She really hates me, doesn't she?" He leans over and plants a kiss on my cheek.

"Hate is a strong word." I lean into his lips, their warmth permeating my skin. "Just be patient. It's going to take time."

Darius nods and leans back in his chair. "I'll just keep showing up."

I glance over at the closed door, the thin window reminding me anyone could walk by and see us. My classroom is on the second floor, so only the squirrels and birds in the tree outside can see in, but even before the day has started, staff are wandering the halls.

"Hold that thought," I say, standing.

I walk over to the door, throw the lock, and pull the tiny shade down. When I turn around, Darius's pupils blow wide as he focuses on my face. I return to the chair, straddling him, and wrapping my fingers around the back of his head.

"You really don't leave the house without a baseball cap, do you?"

"Nope. Only take it off . . ."

"In bed." I ghost my lips over his, and his minty breath fills my nostrils.

"And to shower." His voice is soft, barely audible.

Darius tips his head forward and captures my mouth with his. I pull him closer, my thumb brushing the plastic clasp of his hat as our tongues tangle. He lets out a soft moan—and that, right there, undoes me. That sliver of vulnerability. Him giving in to the kiss. To me. I realize I'm grinding against him slightly—and he's clearly just as affected.

"Coach." I pause the kiss, but leave my lips near his. "If my class weren't arriving in five minutes, I'd be taking care of this."

I reach back with a hand and run my fingers over his tented track pants. Through the thin fabric, my thumb catches the head and adds a little pressure. Darius throws his head back, exhaling, and I lean over and kiss his neck. He's freshly showered, and between his mountain spring freshness and rock-hard cock, my own pants have become a little snug.

Our fun is interrupted by the two-minute bell, and I pull back. But Darius takes my hands, holding me in place.

"Harry, will you go on another date with me?"

"The finals are this weekend." I give his hands a little squeeze. "I'm expecting we'll share a room again."

"Damn right we will, but I can't wait all week." He lifts my hand and kisses my knuckles. "Are we still on for the Mariners game on Wednesday night?"

"An opportunity to gape at sailors? What exactly are we watching them do? Push around some crates on a shipping container? Yell 'Aye Aye Captain' while walking the plank?"

"Uh, no . . . it's a hockey game."

"Oh, so they stick it to each other and puck around the ice? Got it."

"You're fucking adorable." He takes my face in his hands.

"Wednesday night. Hmm. I had very important plans to stay home and read."

"Harry, please. Come with me."

"Dinner first?"

"I'll take you for wings. Give you the full experience." He grins, looking so pleased with himself.

"Alright, fine. But if anyone asks, I'm going for the wings, not the sports."

"Sure, Peterson. Whatever you say."

I stand and extend my hand to him, helping him to his feet. As he rises, he leans in, pressing a soft peck to my cheek. It's quick, but it lingers in the air between us as he turns toward the door, a quiet smile playing on his lips.

If more hockey means more Darius, then I guess it's more hockey for me.

16

HARRY

THERE'S A GIANT, avocado-sized pit in my stomach as I follow Darius down a side street in downtown Portland. It's one of the small ones I've walked a million times but never really paid much attention to. I couldn't tell you the name of the street or any of the shops on it, but I can tell you it's four blocks from the library. He's taking me to some place he swears has "the best wings in the city." I've never been. Or heard of it. *Wing connoisseur* isn't a title I aspire to. But I'm trying to be open-minded. Darius has been nothing but kind to me since Rhode Island, so the least I can do is pretend I didn't pack little pink chewable tablets in anticipation of the nightmare these wings will do on my stomach. The recommended dose is two. I've got six. He's probably going to need them, too.

Darius smiles sweetly and grabs the door, holding it open for me. I'm not usually one to fall for the gentlemanly schtick, but in his case, I'm buying it hook, line, and sinker. He's wearing only part of his uniform—the tracksuit jacket. He's replaced the coordinating pants with jeans. Which I think is his attempt at being slightly more dressed up. It's ridiculous. And totally hot.

Entering The Sauce Boss, the aroma of condiments and fried food smacks me like a flavor explosion to the face. The noise makes the hairs on the back of my neck prickle—people laughing, shouting at the TVs mounted on every wall in the place, the clink of bottles and silverware. These are not my people.

Darius fits right in.

And I fit with Darius.

He takes my hand, pulling me to a high top in the corner. I'm not a betting man, but if I were, I'd bet the house we're the only queer folks in here. And yet, Darius doesn't seem to care about the tiny display of public affection.

He holds the chair out for me, and I really could get used to this kind of doting.

The waitress comes over and hands us water and menus. Mine is sticky, and I sure hope it's hot sauce. "Be back in a few, boys."

I shoot Darius a look. "This is your idea of fine dining?"

"Settle down, Peterson. It may not be fancy, but it's delicious. Trust me."

Trust him. What I've been pushing myself to do for the last week. I'm here. Having wings. About to go to a professional sports game. I've clearly crossed the threshold.

"Yeah. I trust you."

He gives me a wink, and I guess I'm a wings guy now.

I glance at the menu quickly, trying to make sense of all the options. I'm totally out of my league here.

Darius catches my confusion and chuckles. "You're looking at the menu like it's in Latin, aren't you?"

"Latin, I could handle. But this?" I hold up the menu, doing my best to avoid the sticky corner. "What's the difference between dry rub and wet wings? And why are there so many flavors?"

He raises an eyebrow. "You've never had wings before?"

"Nope. You're looking at a rookie." I laugh awkwardly.

He leans back in his seat, a thoughtful look crossing his face. "Alright, Peterson. I got you. Let's start simple. Wings. Buffalo sauce. Mild or medium?"

"Mild," I say quickly, patting the medicine in my pocket.

When the waitress returns, Darius nods and she leans down to hear him over the noise. He orders for us, which strangely makes my insides simmer.

The food arrives fairly fast, which is a blessing, as I'm starving.

"Go on," Darius prods. "They won't bite you. Actually, you're supposed to bite them."

He laughs at himself, and feeling brave, I take my first taste, and—wow.

"Well?" He's holding a wing but hasn't taken a bite yet.

The flavor floats around in my mouth. It's crispy on the outside, juicy on the inside, and the sauce? It's the perfect balance of sweetness and heat without burning my mouth.

"These are . . ." I take another small bite. "Ridiculously good."

With a closed-lip smile, Darius slowly nods as he watches me eat. "Told you."

He takes a small bite, the satisfaction of flavor washing over his face. "You gotta trust me more often, Harry."

I roll my eyes but smile as the flavor bomb continues detonating in my mouth. Darius has a way of making me feel at ease, even when something is outside my comfort zone. At the semi-final game. In the hotel room. On the ice rink. At my apartment. I've never had a thing for guys like him. Athletic guys. Sports guys. Guys who wear baseball hats like their head will float away without it. But with him, I can't deny it. He's sweet, kind, and completely unique to anyone I've ever known.

We finish the basket of wings, and when the waitress brings the check, I grab it and take my wallet out.

"Harry, no." Darius reaches for the check, but I pull it back. "Let me get it."

"You bought the tickets. Dinner's on me."

And then he stands. He's next to me, and even though I'm sitting, we're still pretty much eye to eye.

"Harry." He holds his hand out. "I asked you out for wings and a hockey game. I want to pay. Let me pay. Please."

"You have to let me take care of something," I say.

"Later." He dips in, kissing me on the cheek and gently taking the bill out of my hand.

His touch is light, but there's something firm in the way he does it—like he needs this. Like letting me pay would somehow chip away at the evening he's trying to build. There's a flicker of something unspoken in his eyes —pride, maybe, or hope—and it catches me off guard.

My pulse quickens as we approach the arena just across the street. It's massive. I've never been, and I'm taking in every single detail. The lights are blinding, and the crowd is buzzing with excitement. The air smells like popcorn, beer, and cold metal. People are wearing jerseys and team colors, faces painted, carrying foam fingers and giant cups of soda. It's like I've landed on a distant planet and am witnessing the ritual of a completely different species.

Darius leads me to our seats, and I can feel the energy of the crowd surrounding us. It's like nothing I've ever experienced before, and I can't help but feel a little out of place. This is all so . . . not me. But so him. Them. Hockey fans. Straight folks. Big, loud, rough-and-tumble.

My father used to take my brothers to games all the time. Not just hockey, all the sports. I never went. I was never really invited. Being here, my body feels off-kilter, as if I'm walking on one of those rides where the floor shifts beneath you.

"Relax," Darius says, as we sit down. He pats my shoulder reassuringly. "It's just a hockey game."

"Yeah, just a game," I mutter, glancing at the surrounding people. Everyone's chatting excitedly, giving high-fives to strangers, laughing. And then, just as I'm about to settle in, I see them.

Two guys approach us. They're big, loud, and

wearing matching Mariners jerseys. They sit next to us, and before I can speak, Darius is up, greeting them like long lost brothers.

"Joey! Chuckster." He hugs them both, but in that hetero bro-hug way that's not too intimate. "Didn't realize you boys were coming."

After they finish, they bump fists, and my stomach swirls. I wasn't expecting his friends.

"Joey, Chuck, this is Harry," Darius says casually.

He doesn't say more. Doesn't mention who I am. And who am I anyway? This is our second actual date—I don't count the hotel room. What would he call me other than Harry? I have no idea if they know Darius is gay. Or who they think I am to him or what they think of me in my button-down shirt and khakis.

"Hey, man," Joey says, giving me a handshake that feels more like a slap.

"I'm Chuck," the other guy adds, nodding.

The three of them talk about the game. Hockey. Making jokes I don't get and I'm just . . . sitting there. I have nothing to add to the conversation, and all I know about hockey was taught to me by ten-year-old Johnny Rodriguez on the bench of the semi-final game in Rhode Island.

I do my best to follow the conversation and show interest, but my mind keeps floating back to the fact that these men are so different from me. The way they laugh, the way they talk, and the way they all feel are so foreign.

I glance at Darius, expecting him to notice, but he's completely lost in the conversation with his buddies. He's joking, laughing along, like he's one of them. Because he is.

I felt so optimistic about the night, but now I feel like an outsider here. Because I am.

The game starts, and Darius settles next to me. He leans forward, intent on the game, but every so often, he pats my leg, alternating between my knee and thigh. Joey and Chuck either don't notice or don't care, but I still worry about showing affection here.

During the first break, Darius leans in close, his arm draping across my shoulder as if he has all the time in the world. I can feel his warmth, and his breath brushes the side of my neck. He grins at me, wide and casual.

"Well, I need to hit the bathroom. I'm going to grab us some popcorn and drinks. Want a soda? Beer?"

I dip my chin, giving him my best teacher look—just the right mix of disapproval and amusement, the kind that tells him to keep it light.

"No beer. Soda then. Got it."

He gives me a little wink before he's off, walking toward the concessions with an easy swagger. But then, just as I'm trying to let out a breath, Joey and Chuck are suddenly near, sitting too close, leaning in like they've got questions that aren't really questions.

"So, you and Darius have been hanging out lately?" Joey asks, his tone too casual, like he's just making small talk. But his eyes—there's something a little too sharp in them.

Chuck nods. "Glad to see it. You. With Darius. How's that going? With the two of you."

I feel my heart skip. It's not that I don't like them—

they're cool, I guess—but this? This is pushing it. Do they know he's gay? I'm not trying to out him. I shift, uncomfortable, my gaze flicking to where Darius disappeared. They don't seem to care. It's just casual, right? But why does it feel like they're waiting for me to define and announce something?

"Yeah," I say, forcing a smile. "We're good." It comes out flat, but what else can I say? I can't explain the discomfort in my chest, or the way their curiosity feels like a weight on me.

Joey leans back, smirking. "Cool."

"Yeah, cool," Chuck says.

I blink, unsure about what just happened, but I think Darius's hockey buds interrogated me. Or their version of it, anyway.

Darius returns with popcorn and sodas for everyone. He passes the refreshments out, and sits next to me again, wrapping his arm around my shoulder as the game resumes.

After the Mariners defeat the Norfolk Admirals to the cheers and excitement of the crowd, we bid farewell to Joey and Chuck and head to Darius's car. It's a cloudy night and without the stars, the darker city streets feel endless as the crowd dissipates the further we walk. The silence presses on me like a weight, until finally, Darius takes my hand as we walk down the empty street.

"You okay?" he asks, his voice soft.

I nod, but it's half-hearted. Watching him with Joey and Chuck—laughing, teasing, high-fiving like they've known each other since birth—brought back a feeling I thought I'd left behind. That twinge of being just outside the circle. Like when my dad and brothers crowded around the TV for game night, talking stats and trash like it was their native language, while I lingered at the edges, invisible. They bonded over sports; I learned how to disappear.

It's not that Darius made me feel that way. Not exactly. But the echoes shook me.

"Yeah," I say quickly, hoping that's enough for him.

We get in the car, and as I buckle my seatbelt, I notice my fists are clenched. My heart races as the weight of the evening presses down on my chest. Darius pulls out of the parking spot, and we head toward my apartment.

After a few minutes of silence, my hands are still balled into fists, my head spins, and the words fly out of my mouth before I can stop them.

"We're too different, Darius." I keep my eyes on my lap. "I don't think this is going to work."

He looks over at me, confused. "What? Harry, what are you talking about?"

I blink, pull my lips in and turn to face him. "The hockey game, your friends—everything. This." I point to his hat. "I feel like I'm trying to be someone I'm not. You're . . . you. And I'm . . . me. And I like you. I really do. But I don't know if we should keep doing this."

There's a thick silence in the car. Darius doesn't say anything for a few blocks. Then, that soft gentle voice of his breaks the tension. "Harry, if you like me, why does it matter if I like sports? Or who my friends are? Or if I always wear a hat?" He reaches up and runs his finger along the bill. "I just like wearing a hat. Always have."

"The thing is, I was trying. Am trying, but the way I

felt in there. With your friends. With the entire crowd. Smaller. Less than. Like I don't fit. I don't like feeling that way."

"Harry, I don't want you to feel that way. Ever. Fuck. I thought we were having such a good time." He takes a deep inhale. "Was it Joey and Chuck? Did they say something when I went to the bathroom?"

"No. I mean, yes, but nothing bad. They know something."

"Of course they do. Just because you didn't have a clue about me, doesn't mean my friends don't know."

They knew. Know. That should make me feel better, but it doesn't.

"It's not them. It's me. I'm just too . . . different."

Silence stretches between us, and finally, we pull up to my place. Darius is quiet as he stops the car and looks at me, like he's trying to figure out what this all means.

"Goodbye, Darius."

I leave the car without looking back, feeling like I'm walking away from something I didn't even know I wanted. And I hate myself for it.

17

HARRY

ON THURSDAY AFTERNOON, I'm sitting in my classroom after school, staring at the pile of essays on my desk. We've been exploring the theme of fear in *Lord of the Flies*, particularly irrational fear, and the stack of papers stares back at me accusingly.

The thought of tomorrow's trip to Hartford hangs over me like a dark cloud I can't shake. We're supposed to leave for the finals tomorrow after school, but I have no desire to go. I'm avoiding Darius, which I know is childish, but I can't help it. I've spent the whole day dodging him, like a frightened mouse.

When I walked the kids to PE earlier, I stopped in the hallway and let them enter the gym without me. It's not unheard of for me to let them enter a special class independently, but it's not typical. And even though the kids have no idea what's going on between Darius and me, I'm sure they were all giving me judgmental looks as they passed me.

I know it's silly, letting those old insecurities about

sports and masculinity get to me. It's unfair to Darius, and I hate that. But I can't seem to shake it—and I can't keep pretending everything's fine.

Christine pops her head in the door. She must've seen me wandering the halls earlier with a lost look on my face.

"You okay, Harry?" she asks, leaning against the door-frame with a curious smile.

I give her a tight smile and nod, but she's not buying it. She steps into the room, pulling the door shut behind her.

"You sure?" she presses. "You're looking a little . . . off. Something on your mind?"

I don't want to talk about it, but Christine can be persistent. I know she's just trying to help, but I'm not sure how much I want to share. Especially after I pushed her to give Darius a chance.

"It's nothing," I mutter, flipping through a stack of essays to distract myself.

She raises an eyebrow. "Uh-huh. 'Nothing.' So, you and Darius are good, right? I thought you two were, well . . . you know, getting along. You went to the Mariners game with him last night, right? What happened?" Her chin lifts as her nostrils flare. "Did he do something?"

I stiffen, and for a split second, I feel that familiar flush of frustration creeping up my neck. I shouldn't feel this way, but I can't help it.

I don't know what I want to say. I don't want to talk about Darius, but somehow, I can't bring myself to ignore her accusation.

"Christine, it's not him," I finally say, dragging my

fingers through my hair. "It's me. I don't think I'm ready for . . . whatever this is. Was. I mean, we're just . . . we're too different. You know?"

She looks at me, confused. "Oh, Harry." She walks in and sits at the table closest to my desk. "Talk to me."

I bite my lip, trying to figure out how to explain it. I think about the hockey game, about how I realized it wasn't just Darius's charm or his smile that I'd been drawn to. It's more than that.

"We're two completely different people with different lives, different interests. Darius is the PE teacher, the hockey coach. He goes to sports events. For fun. And I'm—well, I'm the English teacher. I like classical music. I enjoy staying home on Friday night and reading."

"He's Travis, and you're Taylor."

"I don't know who you're talking about, but sure."

"Oh, sweetie." She pats my knee.

"He wears a baseball hat everywhere, and I don't even own a baseball hat."

"I mean, it would be a crime to cover those curls." She offers a smirk.

"We're just . . . too different, Christine," I say, shaking my head. "I thought I could make it work, but I can't. I realized it at the game last night. It's not him—it's me. Sports make me—I don't know—really uncomfortable. It was different with the kids. They're little. We were there to help them. This wasn't like that. This was . . ."

"Super hetero?"

"Exactly." I sigh, wishing the unease in my chest to settle. "I don't think I'm able to see past our differences."

She looks at me with a mixture of sympathy and frustration. "Able to, or don't want to?" she asks softly, crossing her arms over her chest. "You've been on two dates. It sounds like you were really connecting. But, it's your life." She shrugs. "Regardless, you need to talk to him. I saw him moping by the office. You can't just leave him hanging."

"I know," I mutter. "I'll figure it out."

She doesn't push me anymore. She just nods, sensing that I need to figure this out on my own.

After a moment, she asks, "But you're still going to the finals tomorrow?"

I freeze—the finals. With my existential crisis taking over, I'm desperate to bail.

"Uh, actually," I say, shifting uncomfortably, "I was thinking I might back out. I just don't think I can do it."

Christine's eyes widen a little. "You mean, you're not going?"

I shake my head. "I was going to ask Darnelle if someone else could go."

She sighs. "Harry, you and I both know nobody is going to take an overnight trip to Hartford with one day's notice except you or Darnelle herself, and we're not asking our sweet principal who's months from retirement to sit on a bus with a bunch of sweaty fifth graders."

"And their sweaty coach." The image of Darius in my apartment last weekend after his practice, in his jockstrap, flashes in my head.

"Exactly." She cocks an eyebrow. "Which is why you're going."

A few minutes later, I'm pacing outside Darnelle's

office. It's almost four, and I should be home reading cobbled-together essays, but I'm here, hoping for a miracle to save me from another bus ride and hotel situation with Darius.

"Mr. Peterson," Darnelle's voice calls from her office, warm yet authoritative, carrying the weight of someone who's seen it all. I straighten up, taking a deep breath before walking into the room. None of the staff knows how old she is, but she's been in education for almost forty years. She carries herself with a quiet strength that makes her seem ageless. Her short, silver hair is neatly tucked behind her ears, and her glasses sit perched on the tip of her nose as if she's always scrutinizing the world around her with a keen, patient gaze.

I sit down across from her, the polished wooden desk between us reflecting the soft afternoon light filtering through the blinds. Her steady, reassuring presence contrasts with the unease bubbling in my chest. I pull my lips in, instinctively, like a student who knows they've been caught just shy of crossing the line. Darnelle's expression remains gentle but firm, the kind of look that says she'll listen but expects accountability.

"What's up, Harry? Everything okay?"

"Yes. Fine. Great. Amazing." Even though I'm babbling, I offer a smile, hoping to distract from my incoherence.

"Wonderful. And you're all set to chaperone the boys tomorrow? I can't tell you how much I appreciate you doing this. As does Mr. Applegate and the puppies."

"Yeah, about that," I say, but I don't know how to finish.

I can't tell her the truth.

She stares at me for a moment, then sighs. "Okay, Harry. Spill it. What's this about? You were a big help at the semifinals. I was told you were—I believe 'invaluable' was the word Coach Hill used. And the boys need you."

I feel a knot tighten in my stomach. She's right. I was fine with it. I did help. But now, I just don't want to go. Not if it means spending time with Darius on the bus. In the hotel.

"I'm just . . . I'm not sure I'm the best person for it this time. I've got papers to grade."

Her neck bends forward, and I slump a little in my chair. "You can't be serious, Harry. Papers? You can take them on the bus. Is that what this is really about? The boys need you. They look up to you."

I glance at her, feeling the weight of her words pressing down on me. She's right, damn it. She's right. I know I should go. But the thought of being stuck in Hartford with Darius . . .

"You know," she adds, "if you really can't do it, I can step in. But I think you should go."

I nod, even though I don't feel like agreeing with her. "No, you're right," I say softly. "I can bring the essays with me. I'll go."

"Thanks, Harry." She offers a small smile. "You've got this."

As I leave Darnelle's office, my mind races with what's coming. I have to face Darius. I'm not sure what to say or how to act, but for now, all I can do is head to the finals and hope I don't make things worse.

18

HARRY

THE RINK IS BUZZING with energy as we file in, the sound of skate blades cutting into the ice and the chatter of kids echoing off the walls. The New England Peewee Hockey Finals. I may have only been to two hockey games in my entire life, but there's a unique energy with this one. The arena is packed with parents, coaches, and bystanders, all lined up along the sides, their breath visible in the chilly arena. The air is thick with tension and anticipation. Both teams dart around in their team jackets, eager to play. This is it. The finals.

To distract myself from the uneasiness in my body, I focus on the boys skating onto the ice in their matching jerseys. I'm not sure who decided a group of fifth-grade boys were best exemplified by sharks, but there's something adorable about the mean-looking creatures on the front of their uniforms. They're trying their hardest to look like warriors out there, which only adds to the cuteness. I know ten-year-old boys never want to be cute, but they're just going to have to deal.

The crowd roars, and I can see how invested they are. Whether they're here cheering on a friend or family member, they're all here for the hockey. Unlike me. *The boys need you.* Darnelle's words echo in my head.

Darius paces in front of the bench with furrowed brows. There are lines on his forehead I've never seen before. He's always intense when it comes to the Sharks, but this is different. It's not only about the game. This is about everything he's invested in these boys. To say he cares would be a gross understatement. Regardless of what happened between us, it doesn't change the fact that he's an outstanding teacher and coach.

I try not to look at Darius too much. It's hard enough to be here, let alone share the restricted bench area with him. Things have been . . . well, tense between us since the Mariners game. The bus ride down was a reminder of that.

When I got on the bus, I saw Darius had a seat open next to him. He had that little smile on his face, the one that used to make me think maybe things could work between us. But I couldn't sit with him. Not now. Not after everything I did. So I sat up front with Johnny. He spent the entire ride talking my ear off, explaining the "interconnectedness" of all the Marvel movies like it was critical information he needed to pass on to his English teacher. His passion for it was . . . a lot. My head was spinning trying to keep up, but it was kind of sweet—how excited he was to share it with me. I guess it was good to have someone to focus on other than Darius. But even then, I couldn't help but feel guilty.

I'm here for the kids—not him. I've made that decision. I've been ignoring him for a reason. And I'm sticking with it.

We are too different. He's from sports land, I'm from English class—he counts points, and I count semicolons.

But I feel bad. I know how hard he's working with the boys and how much he cares, and perhaps that's why I'm regretting avoiding him. The way he is with these kids—it's something special. Something I didn't expect to see, but now I can't look away. I catch myself glancing over at him, watching him crouch down to give instructions to Johnny, who's bouncing on his skates, ready to jump in. The way Darius's voice is soft, calm, patient—so different from the man I thought I knew before Rhode Island. So similar to the one he began to reveal to me.

The game unfolds with the excitement ten-year-old boys bring to most activities. Fans cheer during the second period, as both the Sharks and the Cougars score. It all happens so fast, I don't even catch the details, but here we are in the last period, tied. The clock has dwindled down to the last thirty seconds, and tension fills the arena as both coaches huddle for a last minute push with their teams.

Darius summons Johnny to his side, but before he goes, Johnny turns to me with wide eyes and a bright grin. "This is it. Coach is putting me in."

"You've got this, Johnny," I say, giving his shoulder a squeeze. "You're the team's secret weapon."

Johnny nods, and gosh, this is why Darius loves coaching them so much. It's not that different from when I'm teaching, and I see a lightbulb illuminate over a child's head when something finally clicks into place. It's those small connections, those *aha moments* that make it all worthwhile.

Johnny lifts his hand to my shoulder, returning my squeeze. "Coach Hill is a good guy. Give him a chance."

I blink, confused for a second. What does Johnny know about Darius and me? Does he know what's been going on between us? Does the whole team? Wait—the entire school? Can he sense the tension between us? My heart skips a beat, and suddenly, I'm not so sure. Maybe Johnny means to give Darius a chance as a coach. A friend. But the way he says it makes me wonder.

Johnny steps toward Darius, who is surrounded by the rest of the team, standing with his whiteboard and pointing to a play on the ice as he explains something. I watch the way Darius interacts with the boys. He's so gentle, so careful. He puts his arm around Johnny's shoulders, leans in close, and for a split second, something in me shifts.

I don't know what it is. Maybe it's the way Darius's eyes are soft when he looks at Johnny. Maybe it's the warmth of the moment, the way the rink hums with energy. I realize something I don't want to admit to myself: Darius has always been more than I've given him credit for. Sure, he loves sports, but he's been patient. Kind. Understanding. He's good with these kids. He's more than just a coach. He cares. And maybe, just maybe, he could care about me, too. If I let him.

The game continues, the tension high. I'm at the railing beside Darius, watching Johnny skate down the rink with the puck. The opposing team's defense is tight, but Johnny doesn't hesitate. He dodges one player, fakes a second, and with a quick flick of his wrist, he sends the puck flying past the goalie. The arena grows silent as it slams into the net with a whoosh. The crowd erupts. With only seconds left, the Sharks have scored.

For a moment, everything goes silent. The ice shimmers in front of me, and all I can hear is the pounding of my heart. The boys are going wild. Johnny's pumping his fists, skating around, and then Darius walks onto the ice, lifting him into the air like he's the MVP of the world. And right now, he is. The buzzer blares and everyone is on their feet. The Sharks won.

The boys are all cheering, throwing their gloves into the air, high-fiving the other team, but I can't look away from Darius. I watch as he steps to the back of the line of boys, and then he catches my eye. He smiles, a little timid, but there's an air of confidence from the game.

"Coach Peterson," he calls out, a hint of that warmth in his voice. "Come join us."

THE LOCKER ROOM is filled with the chaos of the boys still buzzing from their win. They're jumping around, making noise, full of energy. The room smells like sweat—and not in the good way. Darius has already corralled them into a huddle, all of them chattering about the game. He stands tall, his arms raised, and within moments, the room suddenly hushes.

"Listen up, guys," he says, his tone firm but proud. "We've worked our butts off to get here. And today, we showed what happens when we trust each other and play as a team. Every single one of you did your part. When it mattered, we pulled together—no one did it alone."

The boys, still catching their breath, look up at him, wide-eyed. Darius's voice softens slightly, a small smile creeping onto his face. "You've earned this moment—every bit of it. So take a second to enjoy it. But remember, it's teamwork that brought us here—and it's teamwork that will keep us moving forward."

The boys stand a little straighter, their earlier chaos settling into something quieter—pride, maybe—as they take in his words. Something about the way they look at him, like he's given them more than just advice, settles any lingering uncertainties. And then it hits me: maybe there's more to this whole sports thing than I ever gave it credit for. Maybe it's not just about winning or the noise or being coordinated enough to catch flying balls or the rules I never learned. Maybe it's about connection. Belonging. Something I've spent a long time convincing myself I didn't need.

But then Darius's tone changes. He looks directly at me, and the weight of his gaze makes my stomach flutter. "On the rink, we work to score on the ice. But what about scoring in life? Trusting in each other, giving each other a chance . . ." His words linger, almost too heavy to bear. He glances at the boys, making sure they're all paying attention, but then his eyes lock onto mine again. "We deserve a chance, Harry."

A lump forms in my throat, his words hitting me harder than I expect. Is he really doing this in front of the team? There are a few parents gathered around the perimeter, and everyone's staring at me. The tension in my chest, which I've been holding onto for days, finally starts to crack.

"Whaddya say?" Darius moves toward me, and that lump in my throat has taken up permanent residence.

I nod and realize tears are stinging the corners of my eyes.

"Go for it, Coach!" Johnny shouts.

I'm pretty sure he's talking to Darius, but I step forward anyway and pull their coach into a big hug, warmth and quiet support radiating from him. The rest of the boys clap and cheer, and I'm momentarily caught off guard by their reaction to his spontaneous words to me. Or maybe he planned this. It doesn't matter. What matters is the deep gratitude I feel—for his hard work with the boys, for his quiet dedication. And that smile, the sweetness he tried so hard to hide—it seals the deal. But mostly, it just feels amazing to have him in my arms again.

Darius pulls back from our hug and shouts to the team. "Okay, boys, who wants waffles?"

They all scream their desire for victory-earned carbs and follow the parents out to the bus.

As the locker room door shuts behind them, the sound of laughter fading into the distance, Darius and I are alone. Finally.

"I'm sorry." The words come out heavier than I expect. "I've been avoiding you. The sports, they trigger something in me. I know that's lame." I lick my lips and look up at Darius, his big eyes so hopeful. "But, tonight, I don't know. I think for the first time, watching you with the boys, I'm starting to figure it out. Or at least I want to."

Darius steps closer, his face soft. He reaches out, his hand brushing against my jaw. "Harry, we're both still figuring things out. But that's okay. We don't have to have it all figured out right now. But I know how I feel about you, and if you'll let me, I'd like to keep showing up. Keep showing you what an amazing man you are." His fingers hold my chin in place. "I want to take a chance. On us."

I nod, my heart racing like a rocket poised for liftoff. "I want to take a chance on you too," I say, quiet but sure. "On us."

And then, slowly, he leans in. And this time, I don't pull away. He kisses me, soft and warm, and for a moment, I finally feel like maybe—just maybe—we've got a shot at this. At something real.

And with Darius on my side, in this moment, I'm not scared anymore. Love is worth the risk. He's worth it. He captures my lips again, and I pull him close, the thrill of possibility radiating between us.

Life is about the shots you take—and I'm not passing this one up.

Darius

EPILOGUE: ONE YEAR LATER
DARIUS

I walk into the apartment, and the aroma of Harry's cinnamon tea lingers in the air. The same scent fills the apartment every evening, wrapping itself around our home like a quiet embrace. The sound of the door clicking shut brings me back to the present, and I lean against it for a second, taking in the familiar warmth of the space.

A lot has happened in the last year, since we won the finals. We didn't even make it to the semis this year, but we had a fantastic season. New boys. New dynamic. Everyone had fun, and that's what truly matters.

Last summer, after dating for a few months, I asked Harry to move in with me. He laughed so hard, I thought he might choke on his tea. "No way," he'd said, shaking his head. "Your place looks like a sad dorm room, Darius. And besides, my bookshelves are non-negotiable." He loves those built-in bookshelves as much as I love hockey.

But then Harry came around. Kind of. He didn't

want to leave his place but didn't want to lose me. So, he did what Harry does—he compromised. He asked me to move in with him, and it was ridiculous, because I had already been given a dresser drawer and a shelf in his medicine cabinet, but I couldn't help the grin that illuminated my face. I mean, it was the bookshelves. Apparently, bookshelves can cause the guy you're wild about to ask you to move in. And now, here I am. With Harry. Together. In his apartment. Our apartment.

Even though Harry's place is smaller than mine, it feels like ours. There's an easy rhythm to everything—comfortable, lived-in. My old place never really felt like home. Aside from a few trophies, it was just a space. This, though . . . this feels grown-up. And I like that. I like living somewhere that feels more like real life. Fuck—I'm an adult, with a place that feels like home, and a boyfriend who's sweet, smart, and sexy as hell.

I grab a bottle of water from the fridge, and head toward the living room where Harry's sitting, his reading glasses perched on the edge of his nose, a book open in his lap. He doesn't look up when I sit down, but I can tell he's aware of me. His lips twitch as if he's holding back a smile.

"Practice went well," I say, stretching out my legs and leaning back. "Starting with a new group of boys is always a bit of a mess, but I think the kids are getting it."

Harry nods, the faintest of smirks pulling at the corners of his mouth. He's wearing a white T-shirt and a pair of my gym shorts and his curls are damp. "They'll be fifth graders soon enough. I'm sure they're coming along well with such an attentive coach. Did you teach them how to pass, too, or is that next week's lesson?"

"Hey," I say, narrowing my eyes at him, "are you using hockey terminology now?"

He laughs softly, setting his book aside, and then glances up at me, his expression softening. "When you're sleeping with the coach, a few things sink in."

"I love you, Peterson." The words fall out of my mouth like a slapshot—fast, unexpected, and with a force I didn't know I had.

Harry leans over, and I notice that familiar glimmer in his eye, the one that makes me wonder how I ever got so lucky to call him mine.

"I love you too, Coach." He nods to the neatly piled papers on the coffee table. "Especially after spending my evening combing over essays on *A Wrinkle in Time*."

I raise an eyebrow. "Sounds like . . . a blast."

"Actually, it wasn't terrible," he says, his lips twitching in that way he does when he's trying not to smile too much. "Some of them had great ideas. Others— well, they still think time travel involves more high-fives than physics, but, you know. It's all part of the process." His lips close in on mine. "And I rewarded myself with a long, hot bath."

I chuckle, shaking my head. "Essays and hot baths. Living the dream."

"Absolutely," he says with mock seriousness. "It's a tough life, but someone has to live it."

I watch him for a moment, the way he's so comfortable in this place, in this life we've built. I've been lucky to find that here. With him.

"I'm glad to be home," My voice is quieter, more sincere. I don't know if it's the exhaustion from practice or just the weight of everything falling into place, but it feels important to say. "With you."

Harry gives me a small, knowing smile. "Yeah. Me too." Then he leans back, his eyes twinkling. "That bath got me all worked up. Thinking about you on the ice."

"With a bunch of almost fifth graders," I say with a smirk.

"Okay, not that part." He tugs at my warm-up jacket. "More you in that jockstrap. Getting all sweaty."

"No shower?" I ask, even though I already know the answer.

Harry buries his face in my chest and takes a deep inhale through his nose.

"Got it," I say.

I'm yanking at my jacket while he tugs at the hem of my shirt. He's got it up just past my chest before his face returns, planting his nose in my armpit. Harry loves his books, but he may love my scent after practice even more.

"Harry?"

He's lost in the moment.

"Harry? Let's go to the bedroom. Please."

His face remains plastered against my skin. "Mmmmh."

He comes up for air with a radiant smile spread across his face.

"Come on," I say, tugging at his hand. "You can smell me better lying on the bed."

We stumble into the bedroom, removing the rest of

our clothes, but I leave my jockstrap on, at least for now. It's Harry's kryptonite.

When he pushes me back on the bed and crawls over me, I know he means business. But I have some ideas of my own.

On all fours, Harry crashes his mouth on mine, his tongue eager to fill my mouth, and those cute little groans spilling into me as we kiss.

My fingers reach for the sides of his face, but they soon migrate to his curls, slowly drying, their familiar softness soothing my skin. The heat between us ignites a spark, and I hold him closer.

"Harry," I pull back. "I want to taste you."

"Oh, do you, Coach? What part of me would you like to sample?"

"All of you."

I glide my thumb along his jawline, tracing the outline of the face I love so deeply it hurts. "But let's start with your dick."

He chuckles, resting his head in the crook of my neck, and the vibrations from his laughter set my insides aflame.

Harry tosses me a pillow, and I fold it in two, propping my head up while he scoots into position. We've done this before and know the play.

Taking him in my grip, the heat of his shaft is electric as his flushed head glistens with a bead of precum. "Fuck, your cock is superb."

"Open your mouth," he says. "Tongue out."

He slaps his dick against my tongue, and I reach under, cupping his balls, the lavender bath soak on his skin filling my nostrils. He takes a turn, smacking his cock against my cheek, chin, and then returning to my tongue. I close my lips around him, and he finally slides in.

"You like it when I fuck your mouth?"

Unable to speak, I nod and let out a sound I hope he interprets as affirmative. Harry reaches back, cupping the stretched pouch of my jockstrap. "You ready to slam me with your stick?"

He runs his fingers over the fabric, teasing. I feel myself almost escaping from the waistband as Harry's thumb brushes the tip. He brings his hand to his face and pops it into his mouth. "Tasty."

He moves his hands next to my head and lifts himself so he's able to plunge into my mouth. After almost a year, I know exactly what he's doing. Harry likes to get right near the edge before I fuck him.

And I'm happy to help with anything he wants.

We've grown so close. Occasionally, a tinge of regret sneaks in when I think about all the years I wasted being an asshat because I didn't know how to simply tell Harry how I felt. But that's the thing about banking time with someone. With each day we spend together, the version of us that existed before fades into the background.

I lap at the sensitive spot right below the head, and the precum becomes more evident as he pounds away at my throat. It's almost time. His balls contract in my hands, and he pulls out, gasping.

"Okay, I'm ready." Harry moves beside me, lying on his stomach, softly kissing my cheek. "Never in a million years did I think you'd have those blow job skills."

"Well, I've had an excellent coach." I extend my left

arm, and Harry places his head on my chest. "Don't move."

I'm up, hoisting his ankles above his head, burying my face in his ass. Kissing, licking, and finally fucking him with my tongue, as Harry's moans fill the bedroom. The bath, the blowjob, my jockstrap. It's all got Harry horny as hell. He's wide open.

"Darius, Coach. Fuck." He grabs onto his feet, allowing my hands to reach down and spread him wider.

My tongue burrows deeper, and, fuck if his ass isn't the sweetest, most delicious treat. I'm jutting in and out while Harry does his best to thrust his pelvis to match my rhythm. My right hand lets go of his butt cheek and snakes up to his cock. He's dripping precum like a soft serve on a July afternoon.

"Darius, please. Your cock. I want it inside me. Now."

I pull back, my face covered in spit. "How do you want to . . ."

Harry reaches over and grabs the lube from the nightstand drawer. "Why don't you just stay here and let me get things started?" He sits up, crosses his legs, and places a hand on my shoulder.

Glancing up at him, I'll never tire of admiring how fucking handsome he is. And knowing he's all mine.

"Sounds good to me." I lift my hips to slide my jockstrap off, but Harry pushes me down.

"Let's leave it on." He tugs the hem of the pouch to the side and my cock pops out, finally free.

"Now, let's get you nice and ready," he says.

He's slathering lube up and down my shaft, running

over the tip, and then, because Harry is always thorough, he even rubs some on my balls for good measure.

"C'mere." I curl my finger toward my face and he bends over, kissing me. "How did I get so lucky?"

"Fortune favors the bold." He keeps his face near mine, the warmth of his sweet breath making my body hum in anticipation as he applies lube to himself. "You were brave that night in the hotel." He straddles me, and I grab onto his ass, spreading him wide. "And that's your reward."

"Peaches and pucks," I say, pulling his cheeks apart even further. "Two of my favorite things."

Harry smiles, and I adjust myself until my cock finds its target and he slowly lets me in. No matter how much time passes, I will never take for granted the privilege and experience of being inside Harry Peterson.

Lying back while he settles, I stare up at his face. His chest. His beautiful pits when he places his hands behind his head and takes in a deep breath. Harry has become my salve for this thing called life.

After a minute, he moves up, pauses, then lowers himself. All the way, as my cock slots into place like a perfect shot.

He leans forward on my chest, pulses his ass up and down, fucking my dick. My eyes want to close, to take in the extreme bliss, but I don't want to stop watching him.

"Everything good?" I ask.

"Amazing. Your cock feels like heaven." His right hand moves behind and grazes my balls.

He's massaging them, but soon moves south,

spreading my hole with his fingers, patting the perimeter, all while he continues riding me.

"Fantastic coordination, Peterson." Craving more contact, I run my hands up and down his thighs. "Ever think about playing hockey?"

"Not interested." A finger slowly enters me, awaking every nerve in my ass. "But I hear the coach is hot. Maybe I could bang him?"

Laughter spills out of me, and Harry brings his hand up to his mouth, spits, and returns to his work. The saliva adds more slickness to the lube, and, noticing the precum dripping from his flopping erection, I grab it and give it a few strokes.

"I heard he has a thing for adorable English teachers." I thrust up, giving him a jolt that widens his eyes.

"Fuck, yes."

He's abandoned our banter, too lost in the sex, and I move both hands to his waist, grabbing tight while I fuck up. Staring up at him. His face. Body. The way his hard cock bounces as he rides me. It doesn't take long for my orgasm to emerge from the recesses of my soul, and I need to tell him.

"I'm close."

"Okay, hold on," He pauses, shifts off me, and then moves beside me on all fours.

This is why I warned him. Harry always has another idea.

"How about from behind?" He's arching his back, and I'm already behind him, taking in the view.

His glorious hole, wet with lube and precum, open and ready—the mere thought of railing him this way, filling him up, makes my dick pulse, but there's something else I want.

"Do you mind lying on your back?"

Harry glances back, a soft smile on his lips. He flops over, hoists his legs up, and I'm over him.

"I want to see your face. Kiss you." I bite my lower lip, but Harry just pulls me close, grabbing my ass as I enter him from this position.

"I love you, Coach," he says.

"Harry, I love you so much it hurts sometimes." I'm inside him, but I haven't resumed fucking.

He reaches up, cups my face, and smiles. And this feeling—studying his face, being inside him, our bodies stacked—I'd like to freeze this moment like a puck in the crease.

"I'm close." He lifts his pelvis, bucking against me, and I remember why I'm here.

I lift my torso, holding onto his ankles, and pound away. With each slam, Harry's smile widens. His eyes open, but they've rolled back. He's close, too.

Letting go of one leg, I grab his cock and stroke. Between fucking and jerking him, I'm working up a sweat, but damn if he isn't worth it.

"Keep doing that," he pleads. "Oh, fuck. Fuck. Fuck me, Darius. Harder. Please. Fuck the cum out of me."

His body shakes, but I don't stop. I can feel his hole contracting around me as thick ropes coat his chest, stomach, and my fingers, and his face, flush and glowing, lights up. This is another way Harry has let his guard down. Lets me in.

As his body relaxes, witnessing him come undone summons my orgasm.

"Harry, I'm close. Do you want me to . . ."

"Keep going, Coach. Bury it in the net."

I laugh at his turn of phrase, pull his legs up, and lean down to kiss him while I complete the play. Harry nips at my lower lip, his tongue skating across my mouth, and I can feel his hole opening up as I plunge deeper, shooting blast after blast inside him.

My moans mix with his, and his hands wrap around the back of my neck. His mouth peppers my face, ear, even my fucking hair.

I roll next to him and bury my face in his chest. We're a mess and need to clean up, but not yet. I need to hold him for a moment. Be held. Be us.

I breathe in the steady rhythm of his heartbeat, grounding myself in his warmth and the safety we've built together. It's been a journey, but damn if every step hasn't been worth it. No words are necessary. We'll have to move eventually, but for now, this—us—is everything. The rest can wait.

Taking my shot on Harry was the best decision I ever made. Because somewhere between the mess and the magic, I stopped just surviving and started living.

And love—real love—was right here, waiting for me to be brave enough to choose it.

Thank you for reading!

Join my newsletter for updates and announcements: www.mawardell.com

Please consider leaving a review on the book's Amazon page or on Goodreads. Reviews are crucial in helping other readers find new books.

Join the fun in my Facebook Group and Instagram.

Follow me at Amazon to be alerted to new releases.

ACKNOWLEDGMENTS

A huge thank you to everyone who supported me through this journey.

To my brilliant beta readers—GG, Zoe, and Jordan—thank you for your sharp eyes, kind hearts, and for making this book better in every possible way.

To the internet, YouTube tutorials, and a few very patient friends who explained hockey to me more than once—you have my eternal gratitude.

And to my husband: thank you for being my biggest cheerleader, my sounding board, and my best teammate. You make every season better.

ABOUT THE AUTHOR

M.A. Wardell lives near the ocean with his husband and cats. When he isn't writing, he's snuggling those cats, reading all the rom-coms, walking to unravel plot points, and taking long hot baths. He loves playing matchmaker on the page and has many more stories planned.

For more information, visit
https://www.mawardell.com/

Purchase signed copies here!

For access to exclusive content and merchandise,
join me on Patreon.

ALSO BY M.A. WARDELL

THE TEACHERS IN LOVE SERIES

Teacher of the Year - Marvin and Olan's story is available now!

Mistletoe & Mishigas - Sheldon and Theo's story is available now!

Napkins and Other Distractions - Vincent and Kent's story is available now!

Husband of the Year - Marvin and Olan's series finale is available now!

LOVE AT LABYRINTH SOLUTIONS

Meetings with Minotaur - Magnus and Jamie's story coming April 2026

BIG BOYS SMALL SPACES SERIES

Marshmallow Mountain by A.J. Truman and M.A. Wardell - Data and Marsh's story out now

Cut to the Feeling by A.J. Truman and M.A. Wardell - Bryce and Emerson's story out now

OTHER BOOKS

Stirring Spurs - Boone and Wylie's story out now

Peaches and Pucks - Harry and Darius' story out now

Download free bonus stories!

https://www.mawardell.com/freebies